PLAYFUL DAD

50 Tips On Becoming A Fun-loving Father

STEPHEN FLOYD

Introduction

There are no shortcuts to becoming a good dad. No pill to take. No book to read, not even this one. Fatherhood is a lifelong process. AS you walk along. AS you sit down. AS you rise up. DAILY work. Just like running or hitting the gym, the more you do it, the more it becomes part of your way of life; it doesn't necessarily get easier, but it doesn't require as much effort to get things rolling IF you work at it every day. It is easier to steer a moving car, right? Get moving on the path to being a playful dad and adjust your course as you go.

Some of you didn't have a dad at all, others had a father who was physically present, but emotionally absent. It will be easier for you, in some ways, to be a good dad, because *anything* is better than *nothing*. However, fatherhood is about loving, living, and *learning* alongside your kids. AND playing with them. If you don't *like* to play, learn! Kids are fun teachers; ask them *how* to play. It is important that you do not shut them down. If they ask you to do something that you find embarrassing or awkward, think about all the times your own parents let you down, and how nice it would have been had they been willing to be embarrassed for you.

Let me introduce you to the concept of 'The Playful Dad.' He is alive deep down inside every father who is too tired to get down on the floor and wrestle with Junior after work. The Playful Dad wants desperately to have his children as his friends, no matter how grumpy he may seem. The Playful Dad may have been worked to the bone and driven to find other ways to show his kids he loves them, but The Playful Dad can be awakened within each of us, if we but try.

There is a serious lack of fatherhood role models for today's young dads. Fatherhood dot org quotes data from the United States Census Bureau claiming that 24 million children in this country (roughly one in three) live without their biological father. That was 2010, and the trend has probably increased that ratio. With nearly half of all marriages ending in divorce, the likelihood that children have good role models for being a father is not high. Now that you are a dad, or soon will be one, you are thinking about how you can be a better father than your Dad was. That is admirable. The Playful Dad is a good father.

Historically, fathers would take their boys out into the field to help with whatever task was at hand as soon as junior was able to help. Whether in an agrarian setting, where Junior would learn how to plant and harvest crops, or in a community of hunters, where the pursuit of meat meant boys would have a 'coming of age,' when they were treated like one of the men, there was a direct line between father and son that has been lost in today's society. On the other hand, dads rarely got to spend time with their daughters in the aforementioned arrangements, and today's fathers have a leg up in THAT regard.

How much a father may have played with his children

in bygone epochs is a matter of debate, since we tend to view survival as more important than play, but since so much play can be used to teach those skills, I am inclined to believe that playtime had an important role, especially with the younger ones who could not join Papa in the hunt or in the fields. Modern children hardly know their fathers, not just because of their living arrangements, but also because of the change in lifestyle that has removed Dad's livelihood from the homestead. How can you take a break to play with your kids when you go away from them to an office for 8 or 10 hours every day? How can you teach them life skills when they are being trained by strangers in everything from basic health and hygiene, like brushing teeth, to how to resolve conflict with bullies? Granted, not everyone can quit the 9-to-5 work routine and start a business or home-school or move into a rural area to practice a subsistence lifestyle, but have you considered what our modern standard of living has done to our children's ability to live well?

Just because you don't recall playing with your father doesn't mean he didn't try. However, do you remember your Dad being playful? Was he serious all the time? Was he able to make a joke at his own expense or do you remember him laughing only when *you* did something? The power that a father has over his children is mind-numbing, especially in the way it echoes through the generations. A father who makes his kids think that he is laughing at their expense is sowing seeds of inferiority that will blossom into a myriad of psychological issues later on in life. But a dad who makes his kids laugh, who plays with them in whatever way he can, who demonstrates an ability to smile in the face of life, this man reaps generations of happiness.

Play

Even if you don't know HOW to play with your kids, it's important that you try. Children are very forgiving if you don't know the rules to their game, whether it is a structured board game or a made-up role-playing adventure using stuffed animals. Simply by showing interest in what they're doing, by getting down on the floor next to them, you are assigning honor to their little psyches and are telling them without words that they are important to you. They are more important than your career. They are more important than the news. They are more important than your own relaxation. Whether you take your little ones outside to play catch or sit at the card table and have tea with "Mrs. Nesbit," your play teaches the next generation so much about their own worth, regardless of any skill that may also be passed along.

The younger the child, the easier it is to keep them entertained; from making silly faces and odd noises, to playing hide-and-seek with your hands over your face, you will find that little ones will delight in the attention you are giving. You may find them laughing hysterically or attempting to mimic your face, noise, or action, even within the first few days of life. Don't be discouraged if the little one just sits there like a lump and stares at you; some kids develop faster than others, and some seem to just soak it all in without ANY response, but the time you are putting in, face to face, is shaping that youngster, as you become a regular, normal part of life. If you add in singing and plenty of touch, from simple snuggles, to hand-holding, to games of patty-cake, your babies will KNOW that you love them!

Once you hit toddlerdom, the games will change in complexity only in how the connections are being made in your child's head. Simple games like patty-cake and hide-and-seek move into full-body mode, as you add in more than just gross motor skills. I find two- and three-year-olds to especially love it when you get down on the floor with them, whether to become a 'horse' to be ridden, or just to lie on the carpet and color together. Matching games can help make connections in their brains, and you will be surprised at how well little ones can do, especially when they don't have the distractions of news and business and interpersonal relationship squabbles that we adults have. Don't be surprised if they win! Don't get angry, either. But that is another issue, isn't it?

Graduating to board games can occur at a rather early age, if your child can read, but even Candy Land can be fun, especially when you have more than two players. It is important that YOU play by the rules, even if your youngster doesn't quite understand them all. If you teach your kids that cheating is okay if YOU do it, then any attempt to undo that later in life will be met with scorn. You show yourself to be a hypocrite if you permit yourself to cheat, even on a silly game, and it is VITALLY important to live out the values you claim to espouse ALL the time. This is one of the reasons being a playful dad is so important, because your kids will see what values are paramount to you when your guard is down. Likewise, don't let your kids cheat! Some dads think it's good to LET their kids win. Personally, I don't. Whether it's a game of chess or Candy Land, I strive to beat the pants off my kids as if I were in a championship game for world domination. Why would I do that? Because it's not JUST about having fun, it is also about assigning value. Your kids will KNOW if you let them win and that will make them feel worse than if they NEVER win when they play a game with you. This is another reason that games of chance, like Candy Land, are so important, because you WILL sometimes lose.

Playing is not just a matter of games, but also of toys. Cars, balls, blocks, dolls, action figures, stuffed animals, anything that can be made to move or build or represent something else; these are toys that dads should use in playing with their kids. And don't just use them as "intended," but use your OWN imagination. Does your toy truck talk? Can your stuffed teddy bear fly? Can you build a tower with balls? This teaches your kids that play is not confined to other people's rules or expectations and unleashes a plethora of pathways into your child's OWN imagination.

50 Tips to Becoming a Fun-loving Father:

Anger

HOW WE DADS handle our anger is very important, not only to the development of our children's own psyches, but also to how they view themselves when they become adults. If we show our kids that it's okay to get out-of-control when something does not go our way when simply playing a game, aren't we communicating that lack of self-control is acceptable ANY time? If, instead, we demonstrate that, even though we may not be HAPPY about a situation, that we handle it in a calm manner, then we can be teaching problem-solving skills that are indispensable later in life AND we inculcate the value of self-control. One of my boys was a real fit-thrower as a youngster. He would toss game pieces into the air, destroy toys that angered him, scream and cry, and generally ruin the experience of playing with him. He did NOT get that from me. What he DID get was the advice, "Control yourself or someone else will have to control you." This is something that we can model for our kids when we play with them. If I get stuck in the licorice while traversing the Lollipop Woods and my child gets Princess Lolly and blows right past me, what would I be teaching if I threw Candy Land up in the air?

A good example

One of my personal strengths is that I generally do not get angry easily, therefore it is much easier for me to talk about keeping your cool than for someone who has a naturally short fuse. That is not to say that I never get angry, but rather, it takes a lot to get me to the place of losing my cool. Some people suggest counting to ten to give yourself time to cool off, but something that works better for me is to get up and walk away for a moment. A word of caution: walking away can look like conflict avoidance, and it can easily become that, especially if you do not return to the situation to resolve it completely. In the moment, however, it is a good way to keep oneself from saying or doing something that cannot be undone. Words are far more powerful weapons than we give them credit for being, and we can wound our kids so easily. Have you heard the expression, "You can't unpluck a chicken?" That is the way words work.

An opportunity to do better

There have been several times when I acted out of anger in a way that was not beneficial for my kids or my relationship with them. One of those times, I yelled 'Shut up!' at one of my boys and the look he gave me was heart-wrenching. Part of why it was so devastating to him is that I so seldom raise my voice at all, that for me to yell showed a real lack of self-control in that moment. I cannot remember what he was saying or doing at the time that provoked that response from me, but soon after my outburst, I asked him to forgive me. I did not realize at the time how huge that was, for a grown man to humble himself and ask his disobedient child for forgiveness for yelling, but I have heard from most of my kids that me apologizing when I am wrong is one of the things they like most about me. Of course, I would prefer to not have yelled in the first place. And that takes practice.

Discipline

YOU MAY HAVE to take a time out of your play when your child misbehaves. Hopefully, simple issues, such as intentionally NOT following the rules or whining when others are winning, can be addressed midstream, without having to pause playtime. However, if the whining becomes a meltdown, or not following the rules clearly becomes a matter of cheating, then you will HAVE to deal with it. Dealing with the misbehavior in the moment is always a better idea than pushing it off until later. First of all, the kids may not remember the incident later. Yes, that actually happens. Secondly, deferred obedience is another form of DISOBEDIENCE. You have a responsibility to your progeny to teach them how to interact with others, even in play, and if your kids learn that they can defer treating others well until it's convenient, or until after they are no longer angry, then they will treat their co-workers, their spouses, and their *own* children that way someday. Lastly, dealing with the issue at the time of its occurrence, even if it interrupts the play time, conveys the fact that actions DO have consequences. If you throw a fit at work, you will most likely lose your job, so it is fitting that if junior throws a fit during playtime, that he should lose the opportunity to play. One caveat; it is important that you, as a dad, do not blow little things out of proportion. For instance, if your daughter whines about you getting to jump ahead to Princess Lolly (what luck!), getting up and walking away from the game would NOT be a proportional response.

A good example

Sometimes isolation is the best response to bad behavior. For some reason, our youngest child seems to have had more trouble controlling his outbursts than most of his siblings. I say most, because I clearly remember our second and third sons having a large number of fits and tantrums over the years. Maybe it is because I am older and more tired all the time that the behavior of our last son seems so egregious. Maybe it is because we slowed down and did NOT discipline him enough along the way. Whatever the case, sending him out of the room when he blows up seems to get him to assess his own behavior faster than any other form of discipline, so much so that he often turns on a dime and tries to avoid being sent out by practicing instant compliance. Of course, the point of the discipline is not simple, mindless obedience, but rather, winning his heart. Allowing him to avoid the consequence of his bad behavior is not necessarily a good thing either. One night recently, as he was playing a game with his sister and his mother, he reacted in an ugly way to his sister, because she was not getting upset at losing. He did not just want to win, he wanted her to feel bad for losing, and the fact that she had a good attitude was really bugging him. In a calculated response, my loving bride ordered him out of the room.

Within minutes, he had calmed down, come out and apologized to his sister, asked her forgiveness and resumed playing the game. I wish this happened every time.

An opportunity to do better

I'm not going to lie; there are many times when I would just as soon quit playing and send the kids to bed rather than deal with discipline. I remember one time, years ago, when the four oldest were quite small, that all of us boys were on the floor roughhousing and one of them (the third in birth order) got angry and hit me on the head. Instead of disciplining him by sending him away, I allowed that incident to ruin the playtime for everyone by saying, 'That's it! We're done!' and getting up and walking away, myself. Now the play was over for the other three boys due to no fault of their own, and a true learning opportunity for the offender was wasted. In retrospect, I could have handled that better. The good news is, whenever the Playful Dad fails, he learns from his failure and does better next time!

Fairness in play

YOU'VE HEARD THE SAYING, "what's good for the goose is good for the gander," right? So if you are going to ask your children not to cheat when you play together, then you should not cheat either. It seems sad that I would have to say that, but I've seen it happen. In order to hasten the end of the time he has to spend suffering through the perceived boredom of child's play, Dad might move his piece closer to the finish line when Junior isn't looking, or dump out half of the tea Mrs. Nesbit had in her glass so he can get up from tea time with his little girl. Not only do you teach your kids that cheating is okay when you do something like that, you also show them that THEY are NOT valuable to you, that you would rather be doing something else, ANYTHING else. Fairness is not just a matter of following the rules; it is an issue of assigning value. When your kids see that you value them enough to play by the rules with them, just like you would if you were playing with a grownup, and when you are not looking to "just be done," then they KNOW that you truly love them because you are treating them as you treat the adults around you, with respect and honor. If you DO NOT treat your co-workers, your friends, and your wife with honor and respect, then I would not expect you to treat your children any differently, and honestly, there is nothing else that I have to say to you. Seriously. You need a different kind of book.

A good example

Depending on my work schedule, there have been numerous days when all I have wanted to do is go take a nap, either right after getting home, or a couple of hours before heading off to night shift. Taking the time to play with one or more of my kids has not always been easy. However, the times that I have sat down to play a round of Trouble or Candy Land or 'Tea,' I have made myself finish the game. The older kids now recognize what I was teaching them by doing so: that I finish what I start, doing what I said I was GOING to do, and that they were more important to me than my own comfort or sleep.

An opportunity to do better

That being said, there have been a number of times when I have limited our play to 'just one round,' in order to keep it very short. Naturally, it was too short for the kids, and why wouldn't it be? I know that my little ones will not always have the time for me later in their lives (cue the song 'Cat's in the Cradle') and that even if they HAVE the time, they may not want to MAKE the time, especially if I have not made the time for them NOW while they are younger. Thankfully, even those times that I have kept the play short have been good times, making connections and strengthening bonds.

Puzzles

MY EXPERIENCE with puzzles has been a mixed bag. Sometimes it can be quite fun to work together on a puzzle, especially when there's a sense of teamwork and you are all completing a common goal. You can have one person working on edges, another trying to assemble a specific image, still another getting all the colors together into piles, and as long as you are enjoying the time together, you are golden! There are opportunities for conversation, you can practice speaking words of affirmation to each other, you will be sharing a sense of accomplishment that is rare in most board games, because instead of just going around a track multiple times, you are assembling a masterpiece that only appears as each does his or her part. HOWEVER, the possibility for conflict is never far off: Where is that piece I just gave you? Who took the edge that was sitting over here? That was MY part! If you are COMPETING over a puzzle, you may be missing the point. Now the togetherness has become a liability instead of an asset. If a pattern is too busy, or if the pieces are too small, or if it's just too massive an undertaking because of the amount of time required, you will end up discouraging your children instead of building them up. And building up your kids is your primary job as their Dad. Being playful should NEVER mean making your kids feel like you are making fun of them.

A good example

There have been a number of jigsaw puzzles that our family has completed together in just one sitting; there have been only a small handful more that we kept out on the dining room table for more than a day or two. As long as we were doing it together, cooperating and not competing to see who got more pieces connected or who was faster, then the experience was enjoyable for everyone. We found that with puzzles that had a greater number of pieces, the possibility for frustration was much higher, and with the smaller puzzles, we completed them too quickly to make a full evening out of it.

An opportunity to do better

As the kids got older, we found it harder to get them all together at the table at once, even for dinner, so puzzle night became much less frequent than I personally would have preferred. Besides that, I found that there were some very competitive members of my family (my wife included) who find it hard not to keep going until the puzzle is complete. Whereas I can get up and walk away from a half-done puzzle and come back to it later (or not), my spouse and most of our brood find it impossible to leave the puzzle out without working on it. Obviously, there has to be some sort of balance that works for YOUR family, but for ours, I felt like it was sometimes easier not to start than to feel like we had to sit there until it was done. I could do better.

Other ways to play

WHEN THE WEATHER ALLOWS, snowball fights can be a lot of fun for everyone, as long as care is taken not to hit a face or intentionally put snow down someone's back. Although it seems like just a few months ago, I realize that that passes very quickly when looking backwards. On the day before my daughter's thirteenth birthday, I had the opportunity to fly up to Anaktuvuk Pass, North of the Arctic Circle. I took her along and she rewarded me with the first snowball of the season. If we did not have a history of snowball fights, I might have reacted differently to being ambushed, but she felt safe enough, even in a place she had never been, to throw a snowball at me. Would your kids feel like they could do that to you without you losing your composure?

Do you WANT to build a snowman? Do it! Even if you are not especially talented as a sculptor, simply rolling balls of snow into larger balls, then stacking them together APPROXIMATES a snowman, and your kids can do the rest. Much like working on a puzzle together, if each of you is allowed to work on something to contribute to the whole, without somebody else micromanaging, you will have GREAT fun in building snow people, or snow forts, or making snow angels. The list of fun things to do in the snow is virtually endless, especially if you are willing to invest in some gear.

Go sledding. There is a hill at the nearby university that we use every year, because it is just about the perfect height. It's not so tall that you have to climb forever to reach the summit, and it's not so short that the downhill ride is over before it began. There is a commercial ski hill nearby that allows you to hold onto a rope, which drags you and your inner tube to the top of the tubing hill. I typically go with the "free" option, even though we have to buy new sleds every couple of years.

In the summer months, mud is your friend. From mud pies to mud fights, to simply wrestling around in a mud hole, remember that mud will wash off and clothes will get clean, but missed opportunities to make memories will never be regained. Here in Alaska, Spring time (or break-up, as we call it) is usually still pretty chilly, and although it is muddy, you will rarely see me playing in it at that time. And if you live some place where water is scarce or expensive, making a mud hole may not be a real possibility for you. I get that. What could you do instead? Getting dirty together creates bonds that do not wash off, even with soap, whereas avoiding the play because it means having to clean up afterward is a very GROWN UP thing to do. As a dad, if you play in the dirt, not only do you show your kids that they are more important than how you come across to other grown ups, it connects YOU with YOUR inner child. I have to remind myself of that when my youngsters TRY to jump in puddles during break-up! Sometimes I even jump in with them.

A good example

Releasing your inner child so that you can honestly play with your kids requires you to give yourself permission to be silly and tell yourself it's okay if someone laughs at you. Just the other night, at my wife's birthday dinner, with all the children, my wife's Mom, and some family friends in the restaurant with us, I made a game of taking the little ones to the bathroom. When we came back, we looked like Monty Python's Ministry of Silly Walks, creating a minor spectacle for the waiters and restaurant staff to smile at. There are some restaurants where this sort of behavior would have been decidedly less appropriate, but I took a chance on a moment of silliness and it paid off with smiles all around.

An opportunity to do better

Part of the curse that comes with the blessing of living in such a technologically advanced age is that we seem to always have our phones with us and there have been a few times that I have allowed my own creativity to be subdued by the easy shortcut of a game on my phone instead of a word game or outside play with the kids. That's not to say that I feel like I should never, ever use a phone or iPad to entertain a child, but when so much magic surrounds us and we take the easy shortcut, it leaves me feeling hollow. The Playful Dad tries to avoid playing with electronics, not just because they may not always be available, but because they short-circuit the creativity that we really want to foster.

Getting physical

EARLIER I MENTIONED wrestling in a mud hole. ANY kind of physical play is important for kids to have with their dads. I remember going into my parents' bedroom on Sunday mornings and climbing ALL over my dad as he was trying to read the newspaper. Mom let it happen (thankfully), although she did sometimes chastise my father for being too rough, usually after I had been too rough with him and he was showing me he was still bigger and stronger than I. There is much to be said for playing horsey or giving piggyback rides (if you can) and for lifting your kids up above your head as if they were flying. Simply getting down on the floor with them and engaging in some sort of playful touch makes a big difference. While some of your kids may have 'Touch' as their primary love language, every single one NEEDS to be touched in order to feel loved. That does not not mean you have to hug them every five minutes. A simple pat on the head or the closeness of letting them climb on you like a jungle gym fulfills that same need. This has been a struggle for me, as 'Touch' is NOT my primary love language; nor is it my secondary or tertiary. I have to **REMIND** myself to hug my kids and I have to **FORCE** myself to let them rub my shoulders when they come up behind me at the computer.

A good example

My oldest daughter has 'Touch' as her primary love language; she shows people she loves them by rubbing their shoulders, giving them hugs, just putting her hand on them. I have learned to allow her to rub my shoulders. I know, some dads are thinking I **WISH** my kid would rub **MY** shoulders, just **ONCE**. But it bugs me. Seriously, I know there must be something broken deep inside me, but I tend to recoil from being touched, even by my own children. SO, instead of cringing away from her, I try to let her massage my shoulders and neck for a few minutes before saying, '**THANKS**, sweetie, that was nice. Seriously, thank you. **THAT'S ENOUGH.**'

An opportunity to do better

All of my kids need to feel my gentle touch more than they do, especially my eldest daughter, as the chief massage-giver in the family. I need to make sure I'm hugging her more often, taking advantage of the moments we have before she leaves the house to start her own family. I know, I know, she's **ONLY** a teenager, I may have many more years before she leaves, but no matter when it is, when I look back at this time in our lives, it will have been over too quickly. How many times have you heard parents lament how quickly the time went by?

Organized play

MOVING on to other kinds of physical play; many dads push their kids, especially their sons, into organized sports. While there may be some excellent memories formed while teaching them how to throw a ball or complete a pass or dribble or shoot or crack the bat, at some point, the coach takes Dad's place and you are relegated to the role of cheerleader. This can also create excellent memories, if you are THERE for the games and your child KNOWS you are there. I have seen entirely too many boys pushed into sports by their fathers who turn it into a metaphor for their very existence when Dad doesn't show up for a game. Be prepared to battle the monsters of your own creation! A son pushed into sport may feel he has to EARN your love. A daughter pushed into sport may try to COMPETE for every man's affection. If you have the opportunity to coach your kids' teams, you will have the added pressure of trying not to play favorite with your child over the other kids on the team. Guess what? You're going to lose that battle, because, as the father, YOUR kids SHOULD be your favorite! I genuinely like my kids. I also genuinely like them

BETTER than yours. Your children may be great, and I'm sure they are, but mine are better. Because I am THEIR Dad, they are my FAVORITE kids in the whole world, and I pick THEM to be on my team over your kids, ANY day, even if your child happens to be a better athlete.

A good example

I had a friend in college whose Dad had been his coach and he had great memories of playing organized sports with his father. I have another friend who went on to BECOME a coach and then had his sons play on the team he was coaching. These father-son experiences seem to have worked well for these families and I believe that there must be some sort of value in it, even though I personally have never been one to engage in team sports.

An opportunity to do better

Perhaps if I HAD spent more time learning how to throw a ball or catch or hit, then I would have been ABLE to teach my kids how to do that. A couple of my boys have expressed a desire to go outside and throw a ball back and forth, but I think a lot of that comes from our cultural expectations that fathers should throw a ball to junior once in a while. If you enjoy doing it, you should do it with your kids. Even if you DO NOT, but they DO, you should give it a go every now and then. My eldest daughter picked up the skill of throwing a football somewhere. I have no idea who taught her, but she has asked me to toss it back and forth a few times, so I have. Of course, she told me I "threw like a girl," and tried to correct my feeble tosses, but at least I was making an effort, and I will continue to do so, as long as she still wants to.

Being athletic

WHETHER OR NOT YOU play organized sports, if you are at all athletic, you will be able to play longer and have MORE fun with your kids than if you are a couch potato staring at screens all day long. Now I understand, some of us are not naturally athletic, and tend toward obesity. I am one of those, myself. But when I decided to lose weight and started running every day, it improved my stamina during play time and gave me another way to spend playful time with my kids. Have you ever taken your four-year-old on a one-mile run? How about doing a 5k with your six-year-old? When your 12-year-old asks if she can ride her bike alongside you on a 6-mile run, you know you have become an athlete.

A good example

When I was in the Army I ran because I had to; when I was training to run the Equinox Marathon, I ran because I wanted to. Now I run because I enjoy it, and my kids come with me because they enjoy the experience of being

WITH me. My youngest son only wants to go if I'm doing a shorter run, and my oldest daughter only wants to go when she can ride her bike, but at least they get outside and get active AND they are spending time with their father in the process!

An opportunity to do better

There have been a couple of times that I have pushed my kids too far on one of my runs, and although there have never been any serious injuries (certainly nothing requiring a visit to Urgent Care), there have been a fair share of tears shed because of my own stubbornness in trying to go too far or too fast for little legs. So I remind myself that spending time together is more important than me getting a certain number of miles in this week.

Camping

SOME OF THE most fun times in my life have been camping with my children. I have taken the whole brood to campgrounds AND to wilderness areas, and both are equally fun, as long as you are safe in how you interact with nature. Alaska is a very wild place, and we have had encounters with moose, bears, and porcupines while camping. I usually begin by having one of the kids help me with the tent while one of the older ones starts a fire. Then we cook sausages or hot dogs over the open flame and go for a walk down to the river after we eat. Typically, this will be followed by telling stories around the campfire, making s'mores and blowing bubbles into the smoke. Did you know that soap bubbles shoot up into the air like rockets when you blow them over the campfire? After a good night's rest (depending on how many strange noises we hear in the woods), I get up first and start the fire and the breakfast, so the kids wake up to a roaring flame and warm eggs and bacon. Each of my kids has mentioned our camping trips with fondness, even though some have been punctuated by drama. Fun fact: if you bring whistles for each of the kids, it will be easier for them to find each other if one wanders off.

A good example

You don't have to LOVE camping to have fun with the kids. My wife is NOT a camper. Somehow, every time she comes with us, it manages to rain. Not just a little, either. SO, we have worked it out, that I will be the designated camping parent. I take the kids, every year. Period. It's just what we do. Because of this, the kids ask about camping even when it is not practical, like the dead of winter. Now it is POSSIBLE to go camping at 40 below, it's just a lot more dangerous and not nearly as fun. And the idea is to try to keep it fun, while also passing on basic survival techniques and just enjoying nature. One time I took the kids out at the end of May and there was still snow on the ground near where we set up the tent. That was a really fun trip because it was NOT in a campground AND we had our dog with us. Elwood was an amazing husky-shepherd mix and he entertained the children while also helping them feel safe. We were just a couple miles outside of cell-phone range, so when the car wouldn't start and I had to hike into range to make a call, it didn't take THAT long, and the kids had the dog, so they were happy.

An opportunity to do better

I mentioned my lovely bride getting rained on every time we've gone camping together. This is one of those ways I could do better, because I can sleep through anything: crying children, rain getting in the tent, children crying

BECAUSE rain is getting in the tent. I did not do well at setting up a rainproof tent AND I did not do well at waking in the night to deal with wet children. Because my dear wife bore the brunt of that burden, she developed an aversion to camping. Who can blame her?

Fishing

THE PLAYFUL DAD takes his kids fishing when he can. Keep in mind, YOU will not be catching any fish during these adventures, as you will be untangling lines, re-stringing hooks, and retrieving fishing poles from the river. Your kids might not catch anything either, but they will remember you as the one who took them fishing. There is much to be learned about the circle of life when you are gutting a fish together, and fish cooked over an open flame tastes better than ANY restaurant fish. Try this: take some bacon with you and fry the fish you catch in the bacon grease. It will likely fall apart into little flakes, which you can mix with mayonnaise and spread over crackers or pilot bread for an amazing treat! And here's a little tip: invest in swimming lessons. Even though everyone in my canoe MUST wear a life jacket, seeing my kids swimming away from a capsized boat is a priceless treasure.

A good example

Some of the memories my kids mention about fishing have little to do with the actual process of harvesting fish. In fact most of the things they talk about are the same sorts of memories they have from camping, but one thing that shines through is the feeling of safety that they got from me. I never rocked the boat to make them feel like they were going to capsize. The times we DID capsize were honest goofs! Even if they ended up in the water, they knew I was trying to keep them safe and that goes a long way in anchoring their souls in feeling safe with their Heavenly Father. Instead of teasing them or mocking their fear, I encouraged them. Literally. I put courage IN them with my words and my actions. Are we far from shore, fighting a fierce wind and vicious waves? I remind them God sees and will help us, but we have to paddle. Instead of just waiting for God to save us when He has equipped us to save each other, I taught my kids to ask God for deliverance and then work furiously to get into a better place. That is a transferable lesson that goes beyond paddling a canoe and applies directly to a number of other life lessons, from getting a job to getting out of debt to getting free of an addictive behavior.

An opportunity to do better

Even though my kids have felt safe GENERALLY on the water, one area I could have done better in is making good calls BEFORE setting out. Like the time I put a 35 horsepower engine on the back of a 12 foot aluminum canoe. We all ended up in the water. God kept us safe, but that was foolish. As Dads, even as Playful Dads, we need to find wisdom in our choices with our little ones.

11

Hunting

LIKE FISHING, most of the experience with hunting has to do with spending time together as opposed to actually harvesting meat. Part of that, for ME, is because of my own lack of hunting skills. My wife calls it "camping with guns." Part of the challenge in hunting with children along, is teaching them how to be quiet. Loud noises are a good way to keep from seeing ANY wildlife. You also have an opportunity to teach respect for life in general. We do not use 'tweety birds' for target practice, nor do we shoot only for sport. There is a place for sport hunting, to be sure, but I am personally of the 'eat what you kill' philosophy. Sometimes having guns around children is looked down upon. Nevertheless, here is an EXCELLENT opportunity to teach gun safety while having fun. Most of my experience at the shooting range was when I was in the military, and therefore, I do not enjoy target shooting. It brings back some very tense memories and the way others behave at the range makes me nervous. I prefer to do firearms training with the kids when we are in the woods, away from people, where we can set up our own targets (old toys and glass bottles are fun). Just make sure you clean up after yourself, so other people can enjoy the woods after you leave!

A good example

The first time a child harvests an animal for food, it is very emotional, more so than anything else, because the power of life and death has been placed in the child's hands. There may be tears. That's okay. Cry along with your son or daughter, because a beautiful creature's life has been sacrificed that your family may eat. I have encouraged my kids to hunt, and we have eaten what they have harvested, from arctic hares to squirrels. No life is unimportant to the Creator and we show Him respect when we thank Him for His creation and use as much of the critter as we can, from meat to clothing, even a fur to display His beauty and provision for future generations to see.

An opportunity to do better

I'm not a good hunter. Maybe it's a lack of practice or a lack of opportunity or a latent desire to let the creatures live and eat dirt instead, I don't know, but the one shining example of a failure while hunting is in NOT letting my sons take the first shot. Maybe it was pride, maybe it was shame, which I guess is a variant of pride, but there have been a couple of times when I have not had enough guns for everyone in the hunting party, and instead of entrusting the 'good' rifle to my son(s), I have kept it for myself, only to NOT have a harvest. That is not to say that my kids WOULD have gotten the game, but I did not give them the chance or show them the trust I could have.

12

Travel

IF YOU CAN AFFORD IT, I would also highly recommend traveling with your kids, whether you are taking them to visit Grandma and Grandpa or enjoying a family vacation. The playful opportunities abound when you are on the road. I clearly remember playing Auto ABCs with my folks when we were driving cross-country. This game requires the players to spot billboards with words beginning with each letter of the alphabet, in order. Another variation has the occupants of the car spotting items along the road that start with each letter, like Apple stand, Birch tree, Campground. If your travels take you into airports, the moving sidewalks and noisy announcements can become objects of play instead of frustration. And if you have the chance to take a train, the opportunities are nearly endless, from exploring the route to the dining car together, to standing between cars and doing funny things with your hair as the wind shapes it. So many times, the stress of travel can make having your kids along a chore, a burden, a torture of sorts, but as a Playful Dad, you can pass on a love for adventure and craft beautiful memories of family togetherness along the way. By the way, it helps if you can schedule your trip so that you are not rushing to make your connections, as nothing ruins a good memory as easily as being dragged through an airport or bus terminal by a little arm. Instead, if you have the time to relax and enjoy a meal between flights, or visit the gift shop at the bus depot, or even grab a hot cocoa together at the train station, the entire experience is enhanced for everyone, and if you can find a way to play, it will be even better.

A good example

When the young-lings were small, we tried to go to Arizona every year to visit with our families. Obviously, flying got really expensive after we had more than four kids, and travel through Canada became more difficult after a passport was required. In recent years, we have managed to take a road trip down to Anchorage a couple of times and the children still speak highly of the train trip we made as a family to Denali National Park for an overnight in a hotel overlooking Glitter Gulch. The memories of having fun together in a new environment really do last a lifetime!

An opportunity to do better

The rush of making connections can easily become a snare that catches your fun-loving spirit and if you use it as an excuse for a grumpy attitude and take it out on the kids, you have joined me and thousands of otherwise playful dads in ruining a trip with our words. It is SO important not to appear grumpy to the kids. On a recent road trip to

Anchorage, I found myself getting irritated with something totally trivial and unimportant. In fact, I cannot even remember what it was that got under my skin. One of my younger kids remarked, "Why is Papa grumpy?" When I hear one of them say I am grumpy, I immediately take it to heart; it's something I'm working on.

13

Building a fort

YOU MAY BE a carpenter by trade or by hobby; I am not. When I decided to make my kids a fort, I had no idea what I was doing. I bought a book of plans (with instructions), then got the lumber and tried my best. I was pleasantly surprised at my efforts, and the original fort is still standing after 18 years. So are the deck and the swing set I added in subsequent years. You don't have to know what you are doing in order to build a great fort, and if you involve and engage your children during the process, you will be building something much much valuable than a playplace. Your children learn a lot from watching you work, especially if that work is directly FOR them. Do you cuss at the hammer when you hit your finger? Do you quit when the beam isn't level? Even if the kids do not play on it every day (here in Fairbanks, NOBODY plays outside at forty below), you will know that your efforts were worth it and THEY will know that you love them through the time you gave them.

A good example

When we first moved into our home in October 2001, there was already snow on the ground in our back yard, but by the time Summer came around, I had planned where I was going to build the fort for the kids, even though I did NOT know what I was doing, during a week when my wife was gone to visit her sister, I took time off from work and built the fort with the 'assistance' of my then 5-year-old and his 3-year-old brother. It was an adventure. And it has withstood the test of time. All seven of the kids have played on that thing over the years and I am so glad I did it.

An opportunity to do better

I intended to build more over the years than I actually did. Sometimes it was financial limitation that wrecked my plan, but mostly it was just plain busy-ness. In retrospect, although I am SO glad that I did build the fort and the swings and the deck and added the trampoline, I wish I had done a little more out there WITH the kids. It is a poor substitute for a father's time to trade out stuff for time, and then expect them to know I loved them because I showed it with the stuff I bought FOR them.

14

The quintessential backyard memory: a tire swing

WHAT IS it about a tire swing? Something about it seems really old-fashioned and evokes imagery of a time gone by, but tying a tire to a tree with a hefty rope is an easy way to make a swing that the kids will really love. You may not change out tires as often as we do here in the interior of Alaska, but I'll wager you know where you can acquire a cheap used tire and some rope. Testing the swing for safety is a must. It is likely that a branch that can hold YOUR weight will also support your kids, but the reverse is NOT often the case. My safety testing has been somewhat lax over the years, and we have had a number of branches broken off the trees in the back yard. Sometimes kids have to learn by trial and error, and a certain degree of allowance is acceptable, if you do not mind a few broken branches. When it comes to broken bones, however, we would definitely like to avoid THAT, so exercise some judgment and keep having fun!

A good example

I was pretty proud of myself for hanging a tire swing in the backyard for the kids. This happened before I had built the full swing set, so for a while, all they had was the tire hanging from a branch in the backyard. I count this as a good example, because I did it; it did not cost much, either in material or time, and it did last for a season or two. If you do not have a tire, you can find something.

An opportunity to do better

This also serves as an example of what NOT to do, as the tree I hung the tire from was technically my neighbor's. Granted, it was hanging into MY yard, and I had a right to ask my neighbor to trim the tree back, but hanging a tire as a swing puts a lot of stress on the tree, and I'm not sure I really had the right to do THAT. I already mentioned stress tests and safety in general: not my strong suit.

15

Imagination

HAVE you ever closed your eyes while someone is reading a story, imagining the scene as it unfolds before your inner eyes? Do you remember daydreaming about what you wanted to do after school or during summer break? Maybe you still do daydream, thinking about your next camping trip or weekend getaway with the missus. Unfortunately, many men seem to have completely lost their ability to imagine anything. They fill their lives with cold, hard facts and figures, and when they get home, exhausted with the toil of the day, what do they do to unwind? On comes the television and off goes the mind. Whether it is sports, comedy, or even the news, the images and sounds that television pumps into your brain provides everything you need and you do not have to imagine anything at all. Maybe your thing is action movies, or video games, or computer puzzles, but rare is the man who retires to his study instead of his 'man-cave,'

Look, I get it. Modern life is tough and you need to relax when you get home, and reading to your mini-me is not at the top of your list. Playing a game that requires imagination sounds even MORE exhausting. And telling a story off the top of your head is not something that can be done spontaneously by many people, regardless of background; that takes practice!

But think about it. If your dad had taken the time to imagine with you, to tell you stories, to read to you, wouldn't it have been great? I remember my dad doing that; not all the time, of course, nor as often as I would have liked, but I remember it happening and how much it meant to me. That is one of the reasons I have tried to make a point of doing it with each of my own kids. I also have come to really appreciate what it meant for Dad to get down on the floor with me, after working all day, even for a few minutes of play, whether to be my horse, or an ogre chasing an elf, or a big old monkey, because as I get older, I find it increasingly harder to get down on all fours and sometimes even harder to get back up.

A good example

One of the good examples I remember with my oldest is taking him on a make-believe hunt. We stalked a stuffed teddy bear and carefully aimed for the heart and lungs, and then the rampaging beast saw us and attacked! We rolled around on the bed, the floor, the couch, scampering around the tiny apartment with the grizzly bear nearly devouring us at every turn. Finally, my brave 5-year-old took the daring shot that ended the harrowing experience. I do not remember ever having as vivid an imaginary adventure with any of the other children.

An opportunity to do better

As I mentioned, the very busy lives we lead these days make it hard to set aside time to activate the imagination which has lain dormant so long in modern man. I know I never duplicated the same level of imaginary play with his siblings as I did with my oldest, and part of that was easily attributed to just being tired. What does it take to be LESS tired? Sometimes intentionally getting more sleep can help, but the older I get, I realize I need more sleep than I did as a younger man.

16

Silliness

YOU MAY HAVE PICKED up on the fact that I can be silly from time to time. (Incidentally, grapes in the nostrils is something only a FEW fathers can pull off...) I highly recommend allowing yourself to be silly. Whether it is your voice or your face or your walk or your clothes, I bet you can find a way to be silly if you give yourself permission. Granted, kids do go through a stage when they are embarrassed by your silliness. That's okay. Power through. Get your silly on. Not only will the laughs you share be genuine, the memories you create will keep the Playful Dad in you alive for years after the kids are out of the house. Then, when your children bring their OWN kids over to visit Grandpa, they will come expecting the silliness to re-emerge, even if it lies dormant for many years in between. Have you ever stretched a rubber band PAST its breaking point? Have you ever tried to balance as many eggs on your head as possible? (Here we go with food again...) Can you gargle the national anthem or recite the alphabet on one burp? Have you ever skipped through the parking lot holding hands? Practice now and your kids and grand kids will thank you.

A good example

One way I practice silliness with my kids is to skip in public. You may have forgotten how fun skipping actually is! Take your kids by the hand as you are walking through a parking lot and tell them you "feel a skip coming on." This way they know you intend for them to join you and you won't be dragging them through the lot. On a count of three, start skipping. Most of my kids join in with me in this silliness, or used to, anyway. My thirteen-year-old decided that she had outgrown it a few weeks ago, but then joined in, anyway, during our last outing to the grocery store. People will stare. You ARE a grown man, after all, skipping through the parking lot! But you are a grown man skipping WITH HIS CHILDREN. This also applies to any other silly walk you may attempt. Be a group of penguins waddling up to the check-out line. Create a line of ducklings following their daddy duck, each one flapping his or her wings just like you. Dance through the aisles while you shop! Make the shopping carts into race cars or construction equipment and make the appropriate noise. How loudly can you "ZOOM?" Can you make your beeping noises loud enough that the people three aisles over are watching out for a forklift? Every stare is accompanied by a smile. Do not be embarrassed. Be proud. You are a Playful Dad!

An opportunity to do better

This is a double-edged sword, because once I have gotten the kids all ramped up, giggling, laughing, snorting, maybe even choking a little on the quantity of grapes in their OWN mouths, it is hard to come back down to earth and get more serious when their mother wants a little decorum at the table. I have failed her multiple times. Knowing how to turn it down a notch or two is something I still have not quite gotten a handle on.

17

Music

PLAYING music is not something every Dad is able to do, and I understand that. I happen to have been awarded the gift of music, playing the piano and the bass guitar around my kids since they were babies. My wife is also very musical, and we sang to our children when they were in the womb, so it is no surprise that each of my children is a multi-instrumentalist and a gifted vocalist. I do not expect your family to be the same. However, even if all you do is sing, with whatever voice God gave you, I believe your children will develop a greater love for music than if all you ever did was play the radio, or had NO music in the house at all. One of my greatest joys has been to play the piano alongside my kids, as another played the guitar, his brother played the drums, and the rest were singing! The memories you will share will be fantastic, whether it's an old hymn with everyone harmonizing, or a Christmas tune sung like Elvis, or a pop tune sung WITHOUT auto-tune!

I also incorporate silliness into my musical interludes with the children, from singing nonsense songs ('Mares eat oats?") to singing an impromptu aria about how stinky the cheese is on the pizza we just picked up from Sam's Club. Bugs Bunny did so much for my music appreciation and my current ability to have fun with my kids with music. I realize now that much of what I was experiencing through Warner Brothers cartoons was actually recorded by Spike Jones and His City Slickers; he called it "Musical DE-preciation." Weird Al Yankovich has done this well with current pop music, making clever parodies that incorporate lyrical mockery and funny noises. You can do this, too, Dad! Even if you don't have "real" musical talent, if you walk into Susie's room and sing about how she has to get ready for bed using the tune of her favorite pop star, it will have a greater effect than if you simply TELL her to get ready. The Playful Dad strikes again!

Even playing the radio while you go about your chores together can have positive effects and make lasting memories. If you cannot agree on what station to listen to, then find one you all HATE and make fun of the music together. I have been able to find something in every single musical genre to appreciate, so it is harder to find a style of music that I actually hate, but there are some styles I like less than others, and finding ways to have fun with the kids over music that no one enjoys can be hilarious. One cautionary note: if one of your kids DOES like the music you are mocking, the results could be nearly catastrophic, especially if your child feels like the family is ganging up in disapproval. For that reason alone, I tend to steer clear of the mockery angle and try, instead, to find something to enjoy about whatever music my kids choose to share with me. Just recently, my eldest, at the age of twenty-one, introduced me to a brand new style of music: German metalcore/electronic dance doing covers of nursery rhymes. The name of the band was "We Butter the Bread with Butter." Not my favorite, but I found something to appreciate about it and praised him for finding something new and very different. You can do the same. When we, as fathers, tell our kids that the music they like is "awful" or "horrible" or use some other pejorative, we are telling them that about their very beings, because music connects with each person in a different way within their souls. Every generation tries to find a way to differentiate themselves from their forbears, and if we reject that, we fuel the rebellion. If we embrace it, we assign value to our kids.

A good example

Thinking of the photos I have with my children sitting on my lap as I play the piano, and then reminiscing over the times I have played either bass or piano with my kids playing drums, guitar, bass, cello, or piano, and hearing them sing along, these are my FAVORITE memories. Now I have been invited to play along with them in some of the songs they have written on their own, and it thrills me to no end.

An opportunity to do better

Sometimes, having multiple musical instruments strewn about the house invites curious fingers to touch and try things they have no knowledge of whatsoever. I regret the times I have reacted in frustration and have asked for quiet. Music is worth more than quiet. Or sanity.

18

Reading and Play

WE HAVE ALREADY TALKED about the importance of reading to your children, both for their mental acuity and their imaginative development. Have you ever acted out a scene you just read? Have you ever recreated a famous story using finger puppets? Have you ever made toys based on the characters from one of your kid's favorite stories? You do not have to have a lot of talent to take a G.I. Joe action figure and dress him up like Gandalf or even Cinderella. One of the most amazing tools in helping a young imagination develop is to take a familiar, old fairy tale and retell it badly. Intentionally put the characters in the wrong location, use modern technology references, make the hero into the villain. As they 'correct' you, encourage your kids to think outside the conventional boxes of traditional thinking. They will start imagining their own twists and turns to the story, and some of it will be quite good!

A good example

With our first boy, I was deployed to Bosnia as a peacekeeper for his first year of life, so I came home to a toddler, not a baby. In retrospect, I realize that much of my intense effort in spending time with him was due in part to a feeling of guilt for not having been there at the start, but one major success in being a Playful Dad came when I would get down on the floor and quote Dr. Seuss with the boy, as we acted out the parts of the story 'Hop on Pop.' We continued this with our second son, and it was a way to both have fun together AND reinforce reading comprehension!

An opportunity to do better

As time goes on, you will find that your energy levels will not permit you to get down on the floor as much as they used to. This happened for me around son number three, so my time acting out stories with *that* son was far less than I had spent with the first two. By the time number four came, I hardly even read to my kids any more, in part because of my age beginning to catch up with me, and in part, because of my schedule at work. I see this as an area where I COULD have done better, because I am no younger, and my work schedule is different, but still demanding, but I try to make more of an effort to play with my seventh child than I did with those in between. Whatever YOUR schedule, remember than no one ever died wishing he had spent more time at the office.

19

Art

NOT EVERYONE IS ARTISTICALLY inclined or blessed, and I do not mean to make you feel bad if you are not, but I guarantee that you are a better artist than your child, at least when they are young. Draw with them. Paint with them. Sculpt with them. Do origami with them. Experiment with the medium and the method and let them teach you things about yourself that you did not even know were latent talents. Once again, I am grateful for the hours spent drawing with my own father, in part for the creativity it awoke in me, and even more so for the memories of time spent together.

A good example

My cartoon rabbits have graced many a fast-food establishment napkin. Granted, they do not serve much purpose, but having your son or daughter look up in wonder when they see the animal take shape before them is worth more than a thousand glowing reviews from jaded art critics. By activating my kids' imaginations when they were very young, I believe I helped foster the artistic spirit that most of my kids have acquired over the years.

An opportunity to do better

It is always possible to be more intentional in ANY area of your life, especially when wanting to inculcate a specific skill or value, like a love for art. I applaud my long-suffering wife for all the hours she spent in home-school art classes having the kids copy different styles of art and encouraging their hand at creativity of any sort. I could have spent more time doing art with the kids, and truthfully, I never really made it a priority. Music WAS a priority; visual arts, not so much. I wonder now what one afternoon a month would have cost me if I had put pencil to paper WITH my kids.

20

Shopping

DO YOU ENJOY SHOPPING? Not everyone does, but as a Playful Dad, you can make a chore into a fun outing. You do not even have to buy a thing. Browse together and talk about the fun things you see in the store. Play around with the hats. Put a piece of clothing on backwards. Ask your kids if you are using a utensil correctly when you clearly are NOT. Take selfies with weird looking fruit. Put your children on a shelf and take a picture that you text to your wife and ask her if she wants you to pick any more up.

My kids seem to have fun when I take them shopping, not because I buy them anything, although a dollar spent here or there on candy or a cheap toy does not hurt anyone, but primarily because we are having fun together, in public, doing something that needs to get done anyway. It can be a chore or it can be a time to be playful!

A good example

For years, I would incorporate our weekly Sam's shopping into my Saturday routine with the kids. I have seen numerous 'memories' pop up on Facebook reminding me of the fun we had, from photos of the kids in carts, to status updates featuring Sam's pizza. Again, it's not the specific activity WHILE shopping that matters, it is the fun you create for your kids along the way.

An opportunity to do better

Somehow, I feel I haven't done as well since Sam's left town and Costco came in. I do not know if it is a matter of not being as familiar with the store's layout, or if I forgot my own mantra and did not make it fun, but the little ones have informed me that they do not enjoy shopping at Costco because I 'go too fast.' The older ones have pointed out that I move too quickly for the little ones to keep up and leave the older siblings to round up the stragglers. I guess that goes to show that we all need to keep on practicing being a Playful Dad and not take it for granted that once achieved, we have somehow arrived and will always BE playful. It takes intentionality.

21

Surprises

JUST ABOUT EVERYONE likes a surprise when it is a happy one. If someone brought you candy at work, or if someone paid for your steak dinner anonymously, you would probably like it. Kids are no exception. The Playful Dad surprises his kids with positive, happy things. Maybe not everyday, because then the kids would begin to expect the 'surprise' and it would lose the positive shock value. When is the last time you surprised your kids with a little note? You could leave it in the lunch box, so it can be found when your child is at school. You could leave it at the normal 'school' table or chair if you home-school like we do. You could even sneak into the kids' rooms and leave notes on their pillows, if you have Dad-ninja moves (I don't). The point of leaving a note is to surprise your son or daughter with a word of encouragement, a sentiment of affection, or some other positive vibe. A note from Dad is precious AND fun.

You do not have to buy gifts to surprise your kids when you get home from work or a business trip. You can find free mementos that can have the same 'I was thinking about you' effect that a note can have, with the added bonus of being a tangible symbol of your care. Once again, if you bring something home every time, it loses the surprise aspect, so I would suggest occasional gifts, just to shake things up. If your primary love language is Giving, or if your kids feel love best through gift-receiving, then you can still give regularly and make the surprise aspect shine through with a note as well.

A good example

Even more than gift-giving, leaving a surprise note where your son or daughter will find it sows seeds of lasting affection. I once put an old mailbox out on the fort in the backyard and I would occasionally leave notes for the kids to find. Like anything, if overdone, it can lose the magic, and if neglected, the cute idea becomes another faded memory, and although I did not leave that many notes out there, the times I did became very special highlights that the boys have talked about for years.

An opportunity to do better

Some of my surprises have gone over better than others, but my biggest regret is in not continuing some of the things I did with the first four, with the last three. Part of it has to do with age and energy, to be sure, but part of it is simply in not being as intentional as I used to be. Thinking about leaving notes for my boys out at the fort made me wonder: when WAS the last time I left a note for my girls?

22

Holidays

THE PLAYFUL DAD makes holidays meaningful and memorable, for the right reasons! We have all heard people complain about how their dad ruined certain holidays, whether through drinking or yelling or just being grumpy. I was blessed with a father who never ruined a single holiday! In fact, MY Dad taught me how to appreciate every single holiday on the calendar. You can do that, too. Christmas offers more play opportunities than most holidays, simply with the focus on toys and music and decorations, but each and every holiday can be celebrated in a playful way. Part of it comes from having a day off that is shared by millions of other people; you can go places and do fun things that you cannot do on 'normal' days, but even if everyone is doing the same thing, you can make the holiday special by developing your own tradition.

A good example

The one holiday I have succeeded in making completely my own is Valentine's Day. When I was a kid, everyone brought Valentines cards and candy and handed them out to the other kids at my public school. Some children got more than others because they were more popular, and some got considerably less, because they were perceived as weird by their classmates. I was somewhere in the middle, but I never liked that feeling of waiting to see how many cards you would get. Later on, of course, the focus changed to romance and I felt left out because I never had a girlfriend to share Valentines with until my senior year in high school. Even then, it felt perfunctory, shallow, and over-commercialized. When I got married, Erin and I made a point of making hand-made Valentines for each other, forgoing the chocolates and the flowers and concentrating on writing down words of blessing for each other. When we started having kids, I took control of the holiday, wrestling it away from the Cupids and the commercialism, making it a day to shower a father's love on his children. When they wake up on February 14th, they find a Valentine (like we used to get in school) and a small box of chocolates from Dad, along with a note of encouragement, usually stressing how PROUD I am of each one. To this day, even the kids who have moved into their own homes get a Valentines Card from THIS Playful Dad.

An opportunity to do better

When celebrating birthdays, the kids have come to expect their mother to buy the presents, bake the cake, do all the wrapping, et cetera. This is an area where I feel like I may have let the kids down a little. I very rarely have had any input in buying their birthday gifts, and it shows. I suppose I am not alone in this, as it is a bit of a stereotype: Dad asking, 'what did I get you?'

23

Pets

DID your dad ever get down on the floor with you to play with your family pet together? Did you ever see him playing with the animal(s) by himself? Pets can be an amazing catalyst for play. I remember seeing my own father playing with the cats, dragging a toy on a string for them to chase. I also can clearly see him in my mind's eye holding the guinea pig, hamster, gerbil, turtle, tortoise, bunny, lizard, each of my pets, actually. For me, I get down and play with the dogs. Generally, we keep our dogs outside, yes, even here in Alaska. They are huskies and get too hot indoors! However, I do bring them in, specifically to play with them and my six-year-old. The girls have played with us, too, but my youngest son seems to enjoy playing with the dogs more than any of my other kids ever have. Whatever pet you have, by playing with your beast, you are showing your kids how to be gentle and kind, how to have fun without being mean, and how to exert dominion over creation, both in your care for the animal and the enjoyment you derive from having it in your home.

A good example

My kids see me taking a sled dog out for a run all the time, nearly every day, in fact, but it is the time we sit down together and play catch with a dog or go out together for a run with the smelly sled-puller that really makes the memories of playfulness. As a Playful Dad, I keep a ball by the back stairs and often invite the younger kids to come down and play with our younger husky, Günter. Watching the dog take flight as he tries to catch the tennis ball midair is amazing for young and old alike. I admit to worrying a bit when the beast blindly jumps down the stairs, making the distance to the ground below a good seven feet instead of two or three, but having a small child sitting on the step in front of me, giggling wildly, calms my trepidation, and seeing the short-haired husky catch the ball triumphantly, even if it means he crashes gracelessly, is a matter of victory for us all.

An opportunity to do better

Sometimes, I admit, it is hard not to get frustrated either with the fur-baby or the human spawn when playing with the pets gets a little too rough. This is not just a matter that I have dealt with concerning my boys; my sweet little girls have also sometimes been too rough with their animals. Being playful must always include being gentle, and I must confess that sometimes having a sixty pound dog jump up on me has provoked a reaction that was, shall we say, less than gentle, and little eyes are always watching. Reminding my youngest son to be gentle with the dog as he is wrestling on the trampoline would be a lot easier if I were always gentle myself.

24

Wild animals

I CAN CLEARLY REMEMBER several times as a child when my father would pull the car over to 'rescue' a snake or some other wild animal from the Arizona highway. Sometimes he would use a fishing pole to lift the snake off the pavement, sometimes his bare hands to scoop up a frightened lizard. Since we did not go camping that often I cannot recall any larger animals, but my dad taught me to enjoy wild animals, not fear them. I remember my dad trying to get close to a moose on our visit to Yellowstone. Living in Alaska, my kids often encounter moose, right in downtown Fairbanks, but out in the woods, my kids and I have had close encounters with caribou, bears, wolves, porcupines, beavers, eagles, owls, and more. As a playful dad, there are ways to engage with wildlife that are not dangerous or illegal, but still feed the sense of wonder and enjoyment for your kids as well as your own inner child.

First of all, it really is not a good idea to feed the wild animals. Regardless of any laws that may restrict such behavior, the fact is that human food is not good for the critters. Even scavengers like ravens and seagulls will have digestive issues if they eat a steady diet of foods meant for human consumption. Moose and other ungulates need the roughage of the plants they find on their own. Squirrels, beaver, and porcupines live on the plant matter that is part of their natural habitat, and when we see them in town, part of the obstacle to their survival is the fact that we have obstructed their trails with paved bike paths and have torn out their food source to put in ornamental shrubbery that they cannot eat. The Playful Dad will be tempted to show his kids that he cares for animals by putting out a dish of food. Instead of putting out fruit for them to eat, why not plant something that will grow each year that is part of the animals natural diet? Fruit may seem like a good choice, because it's plants, right? But most of the fruit we get in the grocery store is of questionable value when you consider the pesticides and possible GMO connections. Besides, fruit is packed with sugar and a wild animal will choose the easy, sweet calories every time, instead of the healthy food they should be eating. I am not a health nut, and fruit is a wonderful treat for wild animals when they can find it, but it should remain just that, a treat, not a regular part of their diet.

Not only is feeding wild animals bad for their health, it can be dangerous. Even a squirrel can become a raging beast if something comes between him and his food. If we encourage our kids to feed the animals, we may be setting them up to get bitten. I have seen eagles swoop down and carry off small dogs, and when I watched someone feeding wild ducks down by the river, I was amazed at how aggressive the water fowl became. Wisdom would dictate giving animals a wide berth at feeding time in general, but wild animals, accustomed to having to grab food and run, are inherently more of a risk.

The last reason feeding wild animals is not a good idea

is quite simply because it domesticates them. What may begin as one father feeding ducks with his kids down by the park may become several families doing it regularly so that the ducks do not migrate like they are supposed to. Then Winter sets in and the ducks who should have flown South are now stuck in the snow, dependent on humans to come down and feed them. This happened here in Fairbanks, so now we have a flock of semi-domesticated mallards that live year-round behind the Carlson Center. It may seem like Heaven to the ducks; no predators, no hunters, warm water from the power plant, and free food from the humans who take care of them. But what if we stop feeding them now? They have forgotten how to migrate. The Playful Dad engages wild animals in a way that preserves their wildness.

We have already entertained the thought of planting vegetation that animals can eat. Why not plant flora that attracts fauna as well? Depending on where you live, whether you have a fence, and whether you have domesticated pets of your own, there are numerous ways to go about turning your property into a playful spot for wild animals to interact with your kids safely. My dad planted trees that provided shade and fruit, not just for his family, but also for the thousands of migrating birds that go through the Phoenix area. Growing up in the desert, we often saw a large number of indigenous species at play in our treetops, but we also saw non-local songbirds, red robins, even the occasional parrot, stopping in to enjoy the oasis my father had created. If you live near a stream or a river, you could plant bushes and trees that attract beaver or muskrats or assorted furry beasts other than birds. Just make sure you don't have a fence that keeps them from getting in and out of your yard safely. We have had moose step right over the small fence we used to have in our front yard. If you have dogs or cats, your children may be introduced to the 'circle of life' by your pet bringing something they have hunted to your doorstep, and if you have chickens or ducks, you may have to explain why the bear or fox broke in and ate them. The Playful Dad is not discouraged by these teachable moments, but rather, looks for ways to present life's tragedies in a way that prepares our kids to grow and become independent adults one day.

A good example

The Playful Dad does not play with wild animals, as much as he plays with his children in the company of wild animals. Camping with squirrels trying to raid the food box and Canada jays (colloquially known as camp robbers) trying to take the shiny objects left laying about, teaches your children a lot about how to care for wild animals by NOT letting them get human food, and it teaches you a lot about yourself, your patience, and your creativity. Bringing birdseed along for your campground nature-neighbors may seem like a good idea, but it can also spread non-native plants and encourage the wild animals to be more aggressive toward future campers.

An opportunity to do better

Like my father before me, I have been drawn to attempt contact with wild animals, and have gotten too close in the past. While I hope my words and advice about NOT feeding the woodland critters and NOT getting too close will be remembered, I fear my actions, however rare, when I DID get too close may be emulated, just as I ended up following in my father's footsteps. One time in particular stands out, when a young moose got into our yard and hung around our neighborhood for several days. One evening, as I was talking with my upstairs neighbor in the driveway, the moose meandered down the street in front of us, stopping to look at our mailbox, as if he were checking our mail. Suddenly he came charging up the driveway and I jumped over the hood of my truck to escape. My neighbor said he had never seen a fat man move so fast! The next day, that same moose charged at our children as they were playing hockey on our quiet little street. I cannot say I TRIED to get close to that moose, but I should have moved out of its peripheral vision as soon as we saw it.

25

Your dad

IN MANY WAYS, we become like the man who raised us. If your dad was absent physically, you will struggle to be there for your own kids. If he was physically there, but absent emotionally, you will find it hard to connect with your kids. That is not to say that it cannot be done. You are not condemned to repeat the past, nor are you trapped by your DNA, it will simply be an area that you will have to work on, whatever perceived weakness you do not want to pass on. I believe this is what the Bible is referring to when it talks about the sins of the father being visited on future generations. You have a choice. You can fall into the pattern your dad modeled for you and not even try to change anything for the sake of YOUR kids, or you can purposefully attack the issue, whatever it is. My own father broke the chain when it came to physical abuse. Whatever issue you are facing, whether something dangerous like this, or something addictive, or even something silly that you do not want to pass on to the next generation, you CAN change the future.

Keep in mind that you are not alone; there are multiple

support groups for those battling alcoholism or trying to quit smoking, and there are also accountability partners available for any private issue you would not feel comfortable discussing in a group setting, from overcoming pornography to how to be a better husband and father. One of the biggest lies that men hear from the world around them is that we have to be strong, silent and solitary. You are NOT alone. If you do not have a church or another man in your life whom you can talk with, skip to the end of the book right now and contact me, and I will put you in contact with someone who is physically close to you who can be your mentor, your prayer partner, your coffee buddy. Picking yourself up by your own boot straps and making a change for the better may be a popular concept for the American male, but it cannot be sustained without a real change in your heart and without the support of other men.

A good example

One way that I have modeled my father in a good way is in his intentionality toward not allowing his generational pattern of abuse to continue. I took it a step farther by deciding at the very start NOT to use my hands to discipline my kids whenever possible. We designated a plastic kitchen spoon as 'the spanking spoon,' and it is what we used to administer discipline instead of our hands. This was good in a couple of ways: first, it gave us time to cool down before any blows were handed out; the time it took to go and find 'the spanking spoon' was usually sufficient so that the anger we (may have) felt had a few moments to subside so that we were not hitting our kids out of frustration or vexation, but were instead judiciously reminding our offspring of their transgression with a measured dose of discipline; and second, it made a clear separation between us as parents and the instrument of correction. My dad would sometimes use his belt to give me a spanking that he was sure would hurt. I clearly remember seeing him get so angry that he would start undoing his belt and the fear of imminent pain would lead to immediate behavioral changes. I learned from his decision to break the cycle of abuse and took it beyond by being sure to never lash out in anger.

An opportunity to do better

Anger is not the only pattern we learn from our fathers. I also learned how to be too busy. The song "Cat's in the Cradle" always brought a tear to my eye, as the fictional father put his son off because of work only to have his son put him off in the end for the same reason. What is even worse is when it is passed down to the next generation. This is an area where I could have learned from my father's mistakes. I know he worked overtime and voluntarily went in on his days off because we needed the money, but as I see myself putting my own kids off so I can meet a deadline or work a few more hours, I question whether it would be better to stay in debt one year longer so I could spend MORE time with the kiddos now, when they need me.

26

Repairs

ONE THING that you may have noticed as you have become a man is that things always need repair. Whether it is a car that has broken down, a door knob that has fallen off, a piece of the wall that someone ran into, or some home appliance that has stopped working, there will always be SOMETHING that needs fixing. It is the second law of thermodynamics; energy is always lost, things are always winding down. A friend of mine calls it 'battling the effects of the Fall.' As a child, if your parents took care of all the repairs themselves, you may have been introduced to the idea of figuring out how to fix things yourself. If they did not, meaning they either hired someone to do the work or just let things fall apart, then it may have seemed like things that were broken just magically got repaired, or you simply got new stuff when the old stuff broke. If your dad showed you HOW to fix things, you will have a leg up in this area, because the Playful Dad teaches his kids that repairs can be fun.

I am NOT a handy man. I have no skills to fix things around the house. I have never enjoyed doing repairs, usually because the task itself looms large in my psyche and weighs down my spirit until I actually start doing the work. Then, as I find my mind challenged (HOW do I fix this without spending a lot of money, WHERE do I get parts that will work, WHAT tools am I going to use) and as I actually get my hands busy DOING the repairs, there is a sense of satisfaction that accompanies the work itself, even if the repair is not perfect. If the item gets repaired in the process, the satisfaction is even greater! Somehow, I have managed to pass on enough of the attitude about tackling the job at hand so that my children who have already left the house are actually doing the work to maintain their dwellings, although I suspect that they got the actual skills to fix things from their mother.

One thing I have noticed about little children, especially, regardless of their gender, is that if they see Dad trying to fix something, they will want to help. Let them. Obviously, they will not have the skills to actually HELP you, but you can teach them, beginning with age-appropriate attempts. The Playful Dad does not brush aside their interest, nor does he allow his kids to hurt themselves with tools they do not know how to use. There is a balance in there somewhere.

A good example

When I was fixing the wall that had been destroyed by several hooligan children sliding down the basement stairs on sleds, I actually had a couple of them pay attention to how I cut the gypsum and attached it to the studs inside the area I had cut out of the affected (read 'shattered') area. I attached mesh and then spackled over the resulting repair with no one actually offering to help, but apparently paying some attention, because a few years later, when one of my grown sons house-sat and watched over his younger siblings while his mother and I were on a cruise together, he repaired another wall that had been destroyed by running a skateboard into it repeatedly.

An opportunity to do better

For me, it's not SIMPLY a matter of inviting the kids to watch or participate; I have to research HOW to repair anything I attempt to fix, THEN get the tools and supplies to do it before I can even CONSIDER asking the little ones to help. If I had it to do over, I would invest in some simple handy-man courses, if such a thing were offered. If YOU have those skills, you are without excuse. By the way, if you have those skills, how much do you charge?

Cleaning up

_____

MUCH LIKE THE REPAIR ISSUE, cleaning up after a task is very important to inculcate in the younger generation. Whether it is a matter of putting tools back where they belong, or sweeping up the sawdust after a drill or saw has been used, making it an enjoyable time will help your kids to not see it with dread or worse, to leave it to someone else. There is a temptation as a parent to clean up after the kids instead of requiring them to clean up after themselves, but if you are going to make the youngsters clean up their own mess, then Dad needs to clean up his mess, too. We have already discussed doing this while camping or otherwise enjoying the Great Outdoors, because we want to leave the area nicer than we found it for those who come behind. Why wouldn't we want that same attitude in the house?

A good example

When my three oldest boys were eight, six and four years old, respectively, I took them camping at Olnes Pond, an area that had been a state-maintained campground but was NOT maintained when I took them. We set up camp, cooked some hot dogs, sat around the campfire for a while, and then went to bed, but within an hour or so, some teenagers started a raucous party a few sites over. The noise continued deep into the night, with loud music, yelling, and even the occasional gunshot. As a Playful Dad, I did not want to lose my cool and ruin the camping trip by getting angry, but it was very hard to get my boys to sleep, and I'm not sure any of us did. Eventually, the flashing red and blue lights of the arriving troopers (I do not know who called; although tempted, I did not) meant the immediate mass exodus of the hordes of teens from their area, through our campsite and into the woods. The party was over and we finally drifted off to sleep.

When morning came and I exited the tent to make breakfast, I discovered beer bottles strewn all over our camping area. After breakfast, I asked my boys to help me clean it all up. Naturally, they did not care for the idea of cleaning up a mess they did not make, but as I explained that there was no maintenance here any more and if we did not clean it up, no one would, they reluctantly got busy helping. Along the way, more than one of them suggested we make noise, just as the teens had done the night before, to wake them up as they had woken us. I explained that the sad reality was that those responsible for disrupting our sleep probably were NOT in the campground any more, and the hapless campers whose tents we saw on the other side of the pond were likely people like us, who had already BEEN disturbed all night long. Bottom line, we cleaned up and left the campsite better than we found it.

An opportunity to do better

Unfortunately, my ability to clean up a campsite has not translated into an ability to keep the basement clean. My tools are scattered in three different rooms, my camping gear is spread out in even more places, and I swear I have things SOMEWHERE that I have not been able to find, so I suspect that I either loaned them to someone or misplaced them in my mess. This is not playful, this is messy.

28

Chores

IF you never had to do chores as a child, the likelihood is that you were spoiled. People who are accustomed to having others pick up after them give off an air of entitled privilege and those who constantly pick up after others are enabling that kind of selfishness to grow, unchecked. Do you want your kids to grow up expecting others to pick up after them all the time? In order to learn responsibility and grow into successful adults, self-starters who take responsibility and who lead others, kids MUST have chores to do. But, in every job that must be done, there is an element of fun. If you heard Mary Poppins singing the start of 'A Spoonful of Sugar,' that was intentional.

The Playful Dad teaches his kids to do their chores with a happy heart. There does not have to be singing, necessarily, like the Disney characters, but there must not be any grumbling or complaining. You set the tone for your household. Do you complain about work? Then you can expect your kids to complain about their chores. Do you grumble to yourself or to your wife about things that do not go your way? Then you can expect your kids to grumble about their chores. Get it?

A good example

From their earliest years, Erin and I have had the kids doing age-appropriate chores. You're only three; I get it, but you can pick up shoes. So, your chore is to pick up all the shoes and put them on the shoe rack by the door. There have been enough times that the older kids have been reminded that even their youngest siblings do their chores, that I have also been encouraged to get my chores done!

An opportunity to do better

No matter what the chore is that you may shirk, someone is always watching. For whatever reason or excuse that I have had that I have not managed to do the dishes, I have had that come back to bite me, "But Papa didn't do HIS chores!" Consistency cannot be underestimated. Making it fun is pointless if it doesn't get done at all.

29

Frolic

HOW CHEERFULLY DO you move about? Do you regularly engage in merriment? What does that even look like? So many people are so serious, all the time, that they would not recognize a session of old-fashioned frolic if it jumped out in front of them and did a silly dance. From skipping through the parking lot while going shopping, to spontaneously bursting into song while cooking, from running wildly through the park in a game of tag, to quacking like a duck for no good reason in the library, there are as many ways to frolic as there are playful dads to try them out. I am certainly not suggesting you disrupt someone else's day, but combating the seriousness in people's demeanor and tone is easy if you try, and your kids will get a kick out of it.

Planned frolic is hard to pull off, because you are putting an element of structure into something that, by its nature defies the rules. Be open to it. Listen for that little voice that suggests breaking into a skip or a dance; it might be junior!

A good example

Just giving permission for your youngster to 'twist off' for a few minutes is a good place to start, but if you can join in with them, all the better! Each of my boys has gone through periods of needing to run around like a crazy man just before bed, to burn off the excess energy coursing through their veins. Occasionally, I have gotten down on the floor with them for some good old-fashioned wrestling. As I have found it harder to get back up, I have gotten down less frequently to begin with, but the other night I invited the youngest to 'get the energy out,' and he proceeded to drop to the carpet and roll around in circles for several minutes straight. What fun!

An opportunity to do better

Especially as I deal with the effects of having my last child when I was 42 years old, I am finding frolic harder to engage in without hurting myself. I feel like I have given William the short end of the proverbial parenting stick. No matter how long it takes me to get back up, I need to get down on the floor with the little guy!

30

Pleasure in life itself

HOW OFTEN DO you personally stop to smell the roses? This is not a hypothetical question. Seriously, how often do you literally take time out of your schedule to smell flowers? Watch a sunset? Get up for a sunrise? Listen to the birds sing? Go fishing? The more you enjoy life itself, as a man, for yourself, the easier it will be to pass on an appreciation for the little things to your little ones. Get out there and breathe in the fresh air and relish the good things the world offers you to enjoy, then go back and take your kids along and show them the good things you wish you knew about sooner.

If you never take time to enjoy the life God gave you, but are always working toward some future goal, what happens if you get sick or injured and are no longer able to take that dream vacation? What if the market crashes and your retirement fund disappears overnight? Enjoy life NOW, and you will be glad later. No one ever looks back from his deathbed and says, "Gee, I wish I spent more time sitting behind a desk."

A good example

When I take my kids on our Saturday outings, I try to take them on back roads where I know I can point out scenic vistas or marvel at the Fall colors or the amazing snowscapes created by the storm that made travel in town so difficult when the plows were late. One of my favorite places to go is Hagelbarger Avenue, just outside of town, on the North end of Fairbanks. There is a pull-out just off the Steese Highway where we can park to eat our pizza and take in the scope of the current season. Just soaking in the view of our city and its place in Nature does wonder for MY soul, as well as my kids'.

An opportunity to do better

Truth be told, if I took more time to relax around the house, or taking the kids into our own backyard, I could be multiplying my effectiveness. It is too easy to get busy on the latest book to record. When I do venture into the backyard, it is rarely to light a fire in the fire pit or to jump on the trampoline or just lay in the grass and look up at the clouds, although I COULD do those things on just about any given day if I made it a priority. Instead, when I go out back, it is usually to attempt to complete a specific task on the honey-do list.

31

Take a walk

NOT MUCH CLEARS the mind of all the stress of the day like taking a walk with your kids. Summer or Winter, whether you are strolling around the block with Fido, or hiking across town to get groceries, getting out in the elements with your children is a profound way of connecting with them. The physical activity is not only good for their bodies (and yours), but it releases chemicals that create a bond between the people participating in that same activity. Plus, getting out of the house gets you all away from the ever-increasing reach of technology and electronic entertainment. To top it all off, if you take all the kids, you are giving your wife a much needed break from being in Mom mode.

Sometimes, as fathers, we take an enjoyable activity and turn it into a task to be completed, rather than a process to be enjoyed. Taking a walk can be exercise, for the sake of GETTING exercise. It can be a mode of transport, instead of racing the other cars to the store. It can also be a walk, nothing more. Can you do that?

A good example

My youngest son asks me regularly to walk to the 'Candy Store' with him. In point of fact, it is a small convenience store with much more than candy, but it gives me an excuse to put life lessons into practice. We usually take the dog, which means I cannot go into the store, so when we get there, the 7-year-old goes inside and chooses the candy he wants based on the amount of money he brought with him. In the course of one visit, he is getting physical exercise (by walking 1.5 miles to and from the store), mental exercise (by doing math in his head and making choices based on getting the most candy for the least amount of money) AND social exercise (by interacting on his own with an adult to conduct actual business). At first, I was impressed at the boy's math skills as a 7-year-old; now I am impressed with the respect he shows the store owner or clerk, whoever happens to wait on him. The walking in both directions is icing on the cake, because we can enjoy the seasons, the weather, and the sounds of the city together.

An opportunity to do better

Sadly, there have been a couple of times that I have taken the kids out on a walk and have taken them further than their little legs could comfortably go. I remember one three-miler in particular in which one child actually rolled her ankle and had to be carried and another was crying, wailing, in fact, because he was so miserable. Balance, as well as knowing your kids' fitness level is important!

32

Tickles

MY DAD often asked me to tickle his feet or his back and I did, but not as often as he would have liked. The love conveyed by gentle, playful tickling is a powerful force. Unfortunately, with the current climate of inappropriate touching, many fathers have stopped touching their kids altogether. How sad. Tickling is a fun, appropriate way to play with your kids. Of course, knowing when to stop is very important. My youngest has a hard time knowing when NOT to try tickling me. He will sneak up while I am sitting at the computer and jab my ribs with his bony little fingers. Or he will thrust a wiggly fist into my throat in an attempt to tickle. Yikes. Trying not to defend myself from attack is hard!

A good example

When a tickle attack is coming on, I always announce it, just in case the 'victim,' as it were, is not in the mood. Plus, the surprise factor can cause unintended consequences, including a fist applied to your face, if you're not careful. I have successfully allowed the kids to tickle ME from time to time, but it is always a choice, because I do not particularly enjoy being tickled, especially since I often end up in a coughing fit when I am laughing too hard.

An opportunity to do better

There have been a few times when the kids have NOT been in the mood to be tickled and I have not always listened as well as I should have, so what should have been a fun and affectionate encounter ended in tears. They were NOT tears of joy from laughing too hard; they were, in fact, tears from frustration at being tickled when they did not want to be, and I was not paying close enough attention. Being in the moment is so important.

33

Costumes

WHEN IS the last time you dressed like a pirate? How often do you put on a costume of any kind? Part of the process of play involves dressing up like something you clearly are not, whether it is an actor playing a role on stage, or the Playful Dad playing with his kids on a backyard adventure. No one is watching. Go ahead and wear that costume!

We are not talking about spending hundreds of dollars on movie-set creature features, but just using things you can find around the house to make costumes. Cutting out masks from construction paper, making armor from a cardboard box, using towels or blankets as capes, or even letting your little girls do your make-up and hair. When you engage in costume-wearing with your progeny and put their creative juices into overdrive, you will be amazed at what sort of characters you (and they) can become!

A good example

One of my favorite things to do with the kids is to visit secondhand stores like Value Village or Salvation Army. The one thing we CANNOT buy is stuffed animals; there's just no telling how well they got cleaned. Clothes, though, can generally be trusted, and I like trying on the hats and assuming different personae while the children laugh. Well, they used to laugh; my older kids give me groans now, but I can still sometimes get a smile. We keep a bin of costume items in the playroom in case they ever get the urge to dress up at home.

An opportunity to do better

The costume bin is actually an area where I could do better. I know it's in there, and I could go put on something silly at any time, but I do not, at least not as often as I COULD. Sometimes I will find a wig and just casually walk around wearing it, but I could be more intentional at play in this area, not just going for the laugh.

34

Dress fancy

I BELIEVE every dad should dress up at least once a month in a setting where his kids get to see what a well-dressed man looks like. Whether you wear a full suit or just a nice shirt and tie, if it is fancier than your daily outfit, that is what I am shooting for. Take your kids out for a nice dinner in fancy clothes. Go see a play. Get your picture taken as a family. Go to church. The point of it is that the Playful Dad makes dressing up fun, not something to be dreaded or avoided.

A good example

When I worked in radio, I had the luxury of being able to go to work every day in a t-shirt and jeans. The sales executives would wear nice shirts and ties with decent-looking slacks. Then Fridays would roll around and the station would have casual wear Fridays, and everyone else would dress like the on-air talent did on a daily basis. Somehow I got this crazy idea to go against the flow and dress UP when all my coworkers were dressing DOWN.

Add to this the fact that I would bring one of my kids to work with me every other Friday, and so a tradition was born, in which my kids got to see me dressing 'professionally' and looking pretty good, too, I might add. One of my sons really took it to heart and would dress up WITH me, showing up to work with me in his own dress shirt, tie and vest. It was precious.

An opportunity to do better

My idea of dressing up to go OUT has not taken root with the kids like I had envisioned. Maybe it was because we had other outlets for dressing up, but I never met the same enthusiasm for dressing up just to go out as I encountered when they joined me for a day at work in my dress clothes. Of course, we DO live in Alaska, where Carhartt's are acceptable dinner attire at any function, from a banquet to a wedding.

35

Tea party

IF YOU HAVE NOT BEEN INVITED to a tea party lately, perhaps it is time for you to invite your daughter to one that you are throwing. That is not to say that your sons would not enjoy a tea party, in fact, it might be a good idea to involve all the kids in play-acting around a social setting, even if it is one that does not resonate with Americans any more EXCEPT as a childhood activity. From finger foods to the right beverage (tea has a lot of health benefits, but you may want to avoid the caffeinated varieties for the kids), from the decorations to the guest list, you can have a couple of practice sessions with stuffed animals, then step up your game and help your daughter throw a REAL tea party for her friends. Or better yet, for Mom. Involve your children in getting the flowers and setting the tables, in making the sandwiches and in brewing the tea. And if your little girl invites YOU to a tea party? Clear your schedule.

A good example

I remember playing with the boys when they were younger and using their stuffed animals to have adventures, usually along the lines of going on a hunt, or a wild Alaskan safari. I think I remember having a tea party with my oldest daughter when she was quite young, maybe two or three. The dolls and animals each had their own, distinct voices, as we brought them to life. Entering into the imagination of a child is precious, and helping them to enter into YOUR world of imagination is even better!

An opportunity to do better

I do NOT remember doing a tea party with my youngest daughter. I do not recall if I was too busy to make it happen, or if she simply never expressed an interest, although I am fairly certain that she HAS had teas parties with her stuffed animals and dollies. The good news is that there is always an opportunity to try again, right up until the day they move out. Even then, while we may not sit around a child's table and play with dolls, there are places to go to have tea, REAL tea! Why not take your adult daughter out for tea?

36

Funny faces

HOW MANY MARSHMALLOWS can you fit in your cheeks? How many grapes can fit between your lip and gums? Have you folded your bottom lip down or your eyelids up recently? What kind of funny face can you make that no one else in your family can? It is truly amazing how excited kids can get when their dad is making funny faces.

I find that grapes fit nicely between my lips and teeth to make my face take on a decidedly simian appearance. How many little apes might you have sitting at YOUR table if all the kids imitate your monkey business? Asparagus stalks become walrus tusks. Carrots can be everything from antlers to a unicorn's horn. Lettuce leaves can make awesome floppy ears. And John Belushi illustrated perfectly how mashed potatoes can approximate a zit. NONE of this will fly if your wife is not on board. However, there are times when Mom isn't around that Dad can have some fun, can't he? Sharing food hilarity in the safety of your own home may accompany a talk on the appropriate venue for such play. Similarly to how balls may be thrown outside, but not around Mom's favorite lamp in the living room, there is a time and place for food play.

Now I am NOT suggesting you make a funny face when your lovely bride is correcting the brood, nor am I insinuating that ANY time is a good time for a silly face to be made. Random, unexpected times are best, because NO one knows when Dad might become a gorilla or a duck or a Martian with that rubbery, funny face of his.

A good example

I have been blessed with an exceptionally elastic face; I discovered this fact in grade school, when I could turn my eyelids inside out, stretch my neck skin to look like I had swallowed a pencil, and touch my nose with my tongue. Over the years, I used my stretchy face to amuse classmates, mock school principals behind their backs, and generally amuse my sister. It was a natural, foregone conclusion that I would be making funny faces at my children. It truly IS amazing how many grapes I can fit in my mouth!

An opportunity to do better

The hardest part of having such an enviable skill, is knowing when NOT to exercise my gifting. I regret to say that there have been a few times over the years in which I have managed to peeve my wife by making faces when I should have exhibited stoic non-attachment or stern disapproval of my children's antics. Truth be told, it was sometimes my OWN antics which precipitated the scolding. There is a time for every thing under Heaven. I have not quite figured those times out yet.

37

Smiles

CAN you make your kids smile easily? Try it. You may have to practice a bit. The more a person smiles, the more positive chemicals are released in the brain. An article from 2012 in Psychology Today lists the positive effects of smiling, both on the person doing it and on those around them. It improves your mood, it makes you appear more attractive, it releases the same chemicals as chocolate throughout your body, but without the calories! So smile at your kids! And get them to smile, because they will feel better physically, emotionally and mentally.

A good example

I clearly remember taking the time to just smile at my newborns. No words, no silly faces, just smiles. Their wrinkly little frowns and blinking eyes soon eased into smiles of their own. I communicated more with my smiles than I feel I often do now with my words. Sometimes I can look across the table at my 10-year-old and just flash a little grin and she will blossom into a sunflower that widely smiles back. Even my teenage daughter will give me a sly smile when I intentionally smile at her first. Give it a try!

An opportunity to do better

It is entirely too easy to let the worries of life weigh you down, so you forget to smile. I wonder why smiling is not a more natural position for our face. Frowning takes more muscles! And yet, this gloomy Gus will often have his own, normally happy kids ask, 'What's wrong, Papa?' If I say, 'Nothing,' I am making myself a liar, since they obviously saw some sort of concern on my face. That is not to say that I want to adopt a plastic smile-at-the-ready that I wear all the time. I DO want to smile more.

38

Laughter

WHEN YOUR DAD laughed out loud at something, how did you feel? If your first thought was a cringe, it is very possible that most of your father's chuckles came at your expense. If you remember him laughing loudly at certain parts of his favorite movie or TV show, or if you can imagine that time when you told him a joke and he chortled with glee, then this is what you should try to pass on to your OWN kids. The playful dad laughs WITH his kids, not AT them. Furthermore, he finds things that are genuinely funny and fosters a sense of humor that does not require someone else to suffer. It is said that laughter is the best medicine, and that is most certainly true, but it is also a preventative medicine, helping your kids to build fond memories of their childhood by hearing Dad laugh loudly and often.

A good example

There have been a handful of times that we have gone to see a movie as a whole family, during which something caught my fancy and I began to laugh. I am not a quiet snicker, or a hushed chuckle. When I am truly amused enough to laugh, I guffaw outrageously for all to hear, even at the back of the theater. Because I do not laugh that often, or maybe because I do not waste my laughs on silliness, but save them for the truly humorous, each of my children has remarked at how much they loved hearing me laugh during the movie. Better even than that are the times when one of the children has intentionally tried to amuse the family and has managed to get me to laugh along.

An opportunity to do better

I do not laugh that often. Part of it is that I have never really developed an appetite for comedy. Another part is that I do not enjoy being manipulated. Whether it is a sad movie that I know is going to make me cry, or some stand-up comedian whose goal is to get me to laugh, I simply do not like having someone else pull at my heart strings. If something is genuinely amusing, I will enjoy it, even if I am not laughing out loud. That being said, perhaps I could have made more of an effort to take my kids and my wife to 'funny' movies so that they might hear the old man guffaw a little more often.

39

Thankfulness

SOMETIMES, as fathers, we pass on the negative feelings we have about work, our neighbors, our finances, without even trying to do so. It comes across in the way we say things as well as in the words we choose when we talk about the circumstances of our day. In order to pass on a spirit of thankfulness to our children, we must first cultivate it in ourselves. That being said, once we choose to focus on the things we are thankful for, we can more easily ask our children to do the same. Many times when I have attempted to play with my kids, I have encountered grumbling or complaining because they wanted to play something else, or did not like the way the game was going that we WERE already playing together. By using my OWN lack of complaint as a model, I then ask them WHY they are not thankful for what they HAVE. This is why it is important to already be modeling the thankful heart; it is much harder to ask your kids to do something you are not doing than to ask them to follow your model. When you, as a Playful Dad, are showing your kids how to be thankful, then you can ASK them to be thankful in the circumstance. You are playing with them and they should be grateful, not grumbling that they are not winning or not playing something else.

A good example

I have tried to vocalize my thankfulness for everyday things as much as for the big things in life. At Thanksgiving, of course, we have made time to express thankfulness as a family, but just about everybody does THAT. I have made it an essential part of my life to express thankfulness to the children when they have done well, when they complete a chore that helps the family, and when they provide something of value. They have also seen and heard me express gratitude to God for what I DO have instead of complaining about what I do NOT have.

An opportunity to do better

My beautiful bride, Erin, actually does a much better job at this than I do. She will spontaneously lead the kids in a chorus of 'Thank You, Jesus, for…' especially when things are NOT going her way. For instance, the dog just got an unexpected visit to the vet and we have to pay for something we had not planned on. You might hear her tell the children, 'Let's do "Thank You, Jesus" and they will break out in thankfulness. 'Thank you, Jesus, that we have a car.' 'Thank you, Jesus, that we have a dog to TAKE to the vet.' Et Cetera. I wish I were as quick to be thankful as my wife.

40

Faith

LIKEWISE, you model your faith to your kids when you play with them. Put simply, faith is trust. In what do you put your trust? What people or person do you trust? Can your kids trust YOU? Faith is not really a matter of belief, because you can believe something is true, but not put your faith in it. Do you believe that airplanes can fly? Great. How often do you get on one? What about small airplanes? And if we factor in bad weather? You see the difference. We have evidence that what we believe is true, and if we ACT on that evidence, we PROVE it.

Intellectual comprehension is NOT faith. That is not to say that faith and intellect are opposed, far from it. The scriptures I trust invite people to come and reason together with God, not to just take a 'leap of faith.' And when we, as fathers, do things that erode our kids' trust in us, we are teaching them not to trust anyone, or anything. This is not to say that we want our children to trust everyone or be gullible, but we DO want them to trust us, right? Do your kids know when you are not being totally honest with your wife about something that happened when she was not around, but the kids were? What if you tell your son that you are going to catch him if he falls backwards, but then you do not? If you do that kind of thing intentionally, you are not just eroding his faith, you are destroying it brutally.

Instead, when you show yourself to be trustworthy, when you are honest and play by the rules, when you show up when you say you are going to, and when you fulfill your promise to play that game that you did not have time for earlier in the day, you are building their trust in YOU and you are demonstrating YOUR personal faith to be reliable. This crosses over into what you say you believe about everything. Kids are amazing at detecting hypocrisy, and if you let them point it out in you and you respond to it well, you are proving your faith to be real and YOUR trust well-placed.

A good example

I pride myself in never letting my children win a game. If they want to beat me, they have to earn it. Games like Candyland and Trouble and Uno have more to do with luck than skill, so it is quite possible that they will be able to beat me in a casual game. But chess? They have to learn how to play and they have to lose a lot before they can beat me. But no matter what game we may play, they know I will never cheat. In the same way, they know I never let them win, so on the rare occasion that victory is won over the old alpha dog, there is a real reason to celebrate. One of the things I said over and over while I was coaching Chess Club is, "Losing is learning." In chess, especially, every time you play someone better than you, you learn something, as you lose the game. That has turned out to be a good life lesson as well.

An opportunity to do better

In the same breath, I can say that the tears shed by my little ones in the frustration of not being able to beat me sometimes made me question my strategy. Perhaps I could have set my own difficulty level a little lower when playing with the little tykes.

41

Transparency

IF YOU HAVE DOUBTS, you should feel free to share those with your kids as well as your firm trust in what you know to be true. Whether it is a certain doctrine, or a specific person, the Playful Dad who is transparent about his doubts and shortcomings will find a place of honor in his kids' hearts. Share your struggles about what the government officials are doing. Invite your kids into a dialogue about how you question what others believe to be true. Let down your defenses and let them know when you are having a hard time with your attitude about work. Are you questioning your decisions? Let them know. Sometimes the greatest strength is not in bearing a burden alone, but in asking others to help you bear it, even your own children.

A good example

A few years ago, when I was let go from my position as a radio talk-show host, I questioned everything for a while. Seventeen years of a career disappeared overnight and I was struggling with my purpose, my future, my friendships, and even my faith. I shared these inner struggles with my kids, and instead of making them afraid of what the future may hold, their faith and words of support helped me! This was not the first time I had shared my own inner turmoil with my kids, so it did not come as a shock to them when I opened up. If you have made a habit of internalizing all of your struggles, then it will likely be harder to open up with your kids.

An opportunity to do better

There has to be a balance, I think, between letting your kids into your private head space and over-sharing. Around the same time as losing my job, we also moved on from the church we had helped to start some seventeen years before. The timing of both of these life events was very interesting, as I started the radio job just a few weeks before starting the new church, then left the church about a month before losing the position in radio. As I expressed my own doubts about where the provision for our needs might be coming from, my younger children offered their savings to me to get us by. I was humbled and embarrassed, as I realized I may have overshared just a bit. Yet our faith grew together as we watched the ways God DID provide.

42

Scatological functions are funny!

ONE THING that I noticed soon after after first son was born is that you can make a baby laugh with a bodily function. Boys are especially vulnerable to this type of humor, whether it is a belch or a fart or an armpit noise. At some point, I suppose a certain amount of decorum may dictate NOT making these noises in public, but blaming your daughter for a really stinky episode of flatulence can make the room erupt in laughter. Take care, of course, not to embarrass her too much, especially not in front of her friends, but when you are alone, especially when she is younger, you should get her to smile with a well-timed scatological function. It is true; men never really DO grow up.

A good example

Just a few weeks ago, I took Günter, the younger husky, along with my youngest two children, on a Saturday outing. On the way to pick up a pizza from the Great Alaska Pizza Company (like Little Caesar's), the dog released a horrible fart in the back seat and both the kids were horribly grossed out. Instead of reacting in disgust, although I did immediately open the windows, I began to sing a song of my own creation about the 'Fart Dog.' This turned a potentially bad memory of a stinky dog into a humorous recollection of the ridiculous song we all began to sing together. Days later, we were still laughing at the mention of 'Fart Dog.'

An opportunity to do better

Unfortunately, when you encourage flatulence in some instances, it is harder to explain why it is NOT appropriate in OTHER circumstances. My darling little daughter has been letting some doozies loose lately, and not just when we are singing about 'Fart Dog.' She has been farting at the dinner table, in polite company, and worst of all, in the car with closed windows. Much like her father, she has immediately begun to laugh at her own noises, AND at my reaction to her stench.

43

Fun at an other's expense

ONE WARNING IN YOUR PLAY: do NOT have fun at your child's expense. Even if you have a bucket full of children and you are only picking on ONE to make the others laugh, you are sowing seeds of destruction for the whole brood. I have seen otherwise good fathers do this; they go for the cheap laugh by saying something derogatory about one of their kids. I do not care how funny you think it is, or how much your child may laugh; he or she is NOT really having fun. It may not come out for years, but what your kids will take away is damage to their self-worth, and a serious question about YOUR goodness. Nobody likes to be made fun of, NOBODY. So do not do it. It's really that simple. I have heard dads say, "They know I'm joking," or "We're just having fun," as if the hurtful words hurt any less because people are laughing. I am very thankful that my father NEVER made fun of me, and I never make fun of MY kids. TEASING them, however, is something I DO struggle with, and I am trying NOT to do that, for the same reason as not making fun.

A good example

Generally speaking, my kids have not known me to pick on ANY of them for any reason. I have seen dads single out one of their kids and encourage the others to join in, but my kids have known they were safe with me. That is a big deal. Your children are a precious gift from God; why would you want them not to feel safe in their identity with you? Ask my kids if they EVER feared being made fun of by their Dad.

An opportunity to do better

If you are like me and you sometimes fail, allowing words to escape your flapping maw, which you wish you had NOT said. Stop. Do not continue to make fun. Back it up and apologize. Ask forgiveness. That's what I do.

44

Don't play MEAN

IT IS NOT ONLY a matter of words that can cut to the quick. If you are playing with your kids and show blatant favoritism towards one, or direct mean actions towards another, you will be tearing down any good thing that could have come from playing together in the first place. Don't be a bully. Don't take a toy for no reason. Don't hide from your kids unless they know you are playing with them. It may sound basic and unnecessary to say, but seriously, don't be mean.

A good example

My kids generally trust me to be nice BECAUSE I have always been nice to them. I suspect most kids expect their Dad to be nice and are hurt when he is not, only learning to expect meanness when he demonstrates that trait more often than kindness. You do not have to be a pushover to play nice; I have never LET my kids win a game, so they know when they DO win that they have EARNED it. When I won a game of Sorry! the other night, I did not rub it in their faces nor did I say or do mean things to celebrate my win. I have seen dads gloat, and it is not a good look on anyone.

An opportunity to do better

A couple of times, when playing with the kids in a department store, like our local Fred Meyer, I have hidden from one or more of my kids without them knowing I was hiding from them. This created a panic, which I did not intend. I did not want to instill fear, only to play, and when my oldest daughter said, 'Don't be mean,' I really took it to heart.

45

Sarcasm

A SIMILAR ISSUE is that of sarcasm. I hate it. When I hear Dads get sarcastic with their kids, I cringe. Just like making fun of your kids, using sarcasm sows the seeds of destruction. Do you want your kids to TRUST you? Then do not lie. Do not use sarcasm and mock them with your tone or your words. Sarcasm undermines trust, and even if your kids act like it is no big deal, I think it IS. Examine your own heart and ask yourself how you would feel if your boss was sarcastic with you. Would you feel VALUED? Would you question your standing? This happens with your kids, as well.

A good example

I have never seen sarcasm used in a good way; even when it is meant to be in fun, it sows seeds of distrust. Because I have never used sarcasm with my kids and have not tolerated it in my house, on the rare occasion that I HAVE responded sarcastically, my own children have called me out on it. The fact that I have been transparent with my children and have welcomed criticism has also helped them feel safe enough to point out any hypocrisy. 'I thought you don't LIKE sarcasm, why did you just say that?'

An opportunity to do better

Words can be hard to master. Our tongues get us in more trouble than any other part of our body. Truly, the ancients had it right when they said that a man who can master his tongue is 'perfect in every way.' That being said, I really try NOT to use sarcasm EVER. If you use it at work, it will creep into your home life. If you use it with your kids, you'll use it with your wife. Soon, you are sarcastic even when you do not intend to be. The other night I sarcastically commented on my wife's driving. That in and of itself is enough to earn a night in the doghouse, but it was compounded by being said in front of the children. And it may not be sarcasm that is your personal peccadillo. Perhaps it is some other slight misuse of your tongue? You hold me accountable and I will do the same for you.

46

Dad jokes

I WAS RECENTLY ASKED by a coworker if there was a class I had to attend when I became a father on how to tell Dad jokes. This was meant as a bit of a slam, I know, but I took pride in it, knowing that even with younger coworkers, my Dad senses were tingling. How do you define a Dad joke? Is it unoriginal? Is it unfunny? Is it corny? I suppose you know it when you hear it, but do not be afraid of telling Dad jokes! Wear them as a badge of honor. You earned it.

A good example

There have been times when I have been on the ball and able to make everyone in the room lose their collective minds with a well-timed bit of humor. I seem to do my best when I have had several cups of strong coffee and I have another middle-aged man in the room to play off. In fact, I have a reputation at work of being able to make everyone laugh. With a little work, I bet you could find yourself making those around you chuckle as well.

An opportunity to do better

If I try too hard, there is no recovering from it. Sometimes, it is really better NOT to try telling jokes, especially if they are not funny. I have severely embarrassed each of my kids at one time or another because of my corny jokes or because I was trying too hard to make them laugh. I have been told repeatedly by my family that I am NOT funny and that I should NOT try to make people laugh, despite having the opposite reputation at work. Is it a perception problem? Are my co-workers only laughing politely?

47

Model play in how you play with your wife

DO you play with your wife? Some men only play with their spouse by teasing, and we have already mentioned how damaging that can be to any long-term relationship. This applies doubly to how you play with your wife. Does she see you as playful and fun? Do you amuse her? Do you sit down to intentionally play a game with her? Does she join you in playing with the children? It is entirely too easy to get complacent in our closest relationships, taking the other person for granted, not doing the things we once did when we were just getting to know one another. By taking the time to play with your wife, you will be making your home that much better for your kids. They will see Mom and Dad enjoying each other and will feel safer in their own position in the family. If the kids see the two of you sitting down to a game of Backgammon or Poker or even Chess, they see you assigning value to each other. Your actions are saying you would rather spend time sitting across from one another, enjoying each other, than playing computer games by yourself or watching something on Netflix. What you play together is not important. HOW you play, however, is VERY important. Are your words kind to one another? Do you laugh together (not AT each other)? Do you play by the rules (no cheating)? When your kids see you playing the same way with your wife that you play with them, they will know, beyond a shadow of a doubt, that you love them. Your kids are an extension of your relationship with your wife. You made them together, after all. When they see that you still enjoy each other and truly care about each other, hearing the kind words you speak to one another and the laughter that you share, then they know that they are not mistakes. Each of us has wondered at some time in our life if we were MEANT to be here. Did you ever wonder if your parents REALLY wanted you? Did you ever question whether they would have been better off if you had not been born? You can head those doubts off in your own children's minds by modeling fun with your wife.

Another way to model play with your spouse is to play together with the kids. Board games and card games offer a structure to do this, but it is also fun to engage in imaginative play as a family. Have you ever suggested that you pretend that you are all on a spaceship together headed to Mars to start a colony? Have you ever taken the family on a pretend camping trip in a tent made of blankets? Have you built a fort under the kitchen table with both you AND your wife playing roles? The possibilities are limited only by your own imagination, and if your wife gets into the creative spirit, the whole family can be transported into a world of make-believe that will build memories for the future that are NOT built by watching movies together.

A good example

Over the years Erin and I have enjoyed everything from board games to assembling jigsaw puzzles to playing cards together at the dinner table. Our children have heard us laughing from the other room as they drifted off to sleep, usually after quite a bit of time doing some laughing of their own. One of the reasons we would stay up and play games together is that we were waiting for the children to fall asleep before we went to bed ourselves. It is a lot easier to poke your head in and tell them to go to sleep if you are on the same floor of the house, after all.

An opportunity to do better

Over the years, it has become entirely too easy to skip the games and just chill out with Netflix instead of laughing together, face to face. It does require more active intention to find the time to play together, and we all get tired and need some down time. That being said, I know that I have taken the easy road far too often and I really WANT to play more with my wife. What would it take to make the time to play a game together, just once a week?

48

How you treat your wife in general

WE ALREADY ADDRESSED the issue of how you play with your wife affecting the way your children see you (and her), but how you treat her in general is also important. Does she feel respected by the children? If not, maybe it is because YOU do not show her respect. Does she feel loved? If you speak words of affection, but act in an unkind or unloving way, your words ring hollow. Does your wife know that you cherish her above all others? This could be the subject of an entire book, just by itself, as you show your kids, and the world at large, what kind of man you are by how much you cherish the wife God gave you. The Playful Dad is a loving husband.

A good example

My adult children have told me that the way I treated their mother while they were growing up influenced how they treated her and how they treat women on the whole. The fact that I made taking her out on dates as often as I could made an impact on them as well. Our relationship wasn't an afterthought or a sidebar to family life; it was central. When the kids were little we managed to get out for a date night once a month. Sitters are expensive, I know; dates can be, as well, but not nearly as expensive as letting your romance sputter under the wet towel of parenthood. As the kids got older and were able to be left to look after each other (another benefit of a large family- the built-in sitters!), we started going out once every two weeks. Now, we manage to get a date night in every single week. My kids see me treat their mom like I really enjoy being with her. Guess what? I DO!

Another big plus is that I have rarely yelled at Erin about anything. It's not that I haven't ever been mad, I just am not generally a person who yells, I guess. I have never thrown things, nor have I punched holes in walls. I remember hearing MY parents argue from the other room, because they tried to keep it from the kids. Erin and I have had our 'fights' out in the open; they have simply been non-violent. This teaches the kids that conflicts have solutions and kindness IN conflict preserves the peace.

An opportunity to do better

We all have bad days. To my chagrin, I have occasionally said things to my wife that I have regretted saying. And to make it worse, I have said these things in front of our dear offspring. If you, too, happen to have a bad day and manage to let words issue from your cake hole that you wish you could take back, then do not hesitate to humble yourself in front of your spouse AND your children and ask her forgiveness IN FRONT OF THEM. That goes so much further than simply NOT saying you are sorry.

49

Affection and fun

WE ALREADY TALKED a bit about communicating through touch while playing, and I want to take it a step farther, because your words also communicate affection, and when you are having fun together, your kids will feel loved, especially if your words match up with your actions. Do you enjoy being together? Tell them that. Do you like them? Let them know. Are your children your favorite kids on the planet? If you communicate that to them WHILE you are playing, then when you have a serious moment and try to say the same thing, it will not come across as hollow words. I could write an entire book on the power of a father's words over his children, but suffice it to say, for now, that when you bless your kids, your words echo through the generations.

A good example

When I think about how most fathers show affection, it usually seems awkward or forced, most likely because those dads never had their own father show them affection well.

I was blessed by a father who would hug me from time to time, wrestle with me, allow me to climb on him, even when he was tired, and even occasionally kissed me. I did not have as much touch from my Dad as some kids had from theirs, but I certainly got more than most, and I have tried to pass that on to MY kids. It is important not to JUST rough-house, but to also show gentle, fatherly affection and one way I have done that well is with my words.

I try to make a point of telling each of my children individually that if I had ALL the children in the world lined up in front of me to choose from, that I would still choose YOU to be my daughter or my son (depending on which one I am speaking with). I tell them EACH you are my favorite __-year-old, depending on how old each one is when I say it. Especially when you have a large family, it's important for the kids not to feel lost in the crowd, as if they only have value as part of the collective. This is one of the reasons my wife and I take the kids out individually for one-on-one dates in a regular rotation.

An opportunity to do better

Blame it on my parents, my Puritan roots, the New England connections my adoptive parents have, whatever the reason, I struggle with showing physical affection. I know a lot of fathers do, in general, but I feel an actual aversion to human touch. This may be another version of the 'Nature versus Nurture' debate. Sometimes one of my kids will be sitting next to me and will casually drape a leg over my leg, or hang around my shoulders and I cringe, not from disgust at the person, but from some weird desire NOT to be touched. I fear that in pulling away, as I often do, that I am subconsciously telling my kid that he or she is cringe worthy, and even though that is NOT the case, even in trying to go back and allow them to touch me, the initial damage has been done in the pulling away. However, I am open about it with my kids, and have expressed a desire to do better.

50

Food

THE PLAYFUL DAD has fun with food. This is not just a matter of playing with the food and the faces you can make. The Playful Dad involves his kids in playing in the kitchen. Is there a regular meal you can make together with the children? Granted, some work schedules keep Dad out of the house past regular meal times, but maybe you can find a weekend or at least a holiday, where you can involve the kids in cooking or baking together. Once again, age appropriate participation is key. Maybe cracking eggs can be Dad's job, but scrambling them in the bowl can be junior's. The more meals you make together, the more memories you will have for a lifetime, and who knows, you may awaken an inner chef in one of your kids.

Mealtime in general is also an important time of togetherness that can be intentional to communicate well with your offspring. Erin and I have had fun telling 'how we got together stories' at the dinner table. One time we told the story of our meeting and deciding to get married as if we were robots on a space station. Another time, we retold it as if we were in the story of Aladdin. Obviously, we stretch the truth a little in the retelling, but the kids know we are joking around and have picked up on the real truth in our story of friends who listened to God telling them to get married to each other.

A good example

For years, I would get up early on Sunday morning and cook a large breakfast for the entire family, involving one or two of the kids in the preparation. This tradition became known simply as 'Big Breakfast,' and each of the children has had an opportunity to learn how to cook real breakfast food, from scrambled eggs to sausage links, from perfectly pan-fried bacon to spam broiled in the oven. Typically, the morning would begin with me getting some coffee and starting the bacon on the stove-top. Then I would gently wake the one who had agreed the night before to join me in the kitchen. Occasionally I would find that my helper had decided against getting up, but usually it was so exciting to get up early with Dad that it would be harder to keep quiet so as not to wake the siblings!

When my helper would make it to the kitchen, the egg preparation would commence. When the kids were younger, I would crack the eggs and my helper would scramble, mixing in the spices as I added them, but as they grew, the kids would invariably ask to crack the eggs themselves, and I would let them. Sometimes that did mean having to fish out eggshells, but the sense of pride inculcated in a child by allowing him to do the work was worth it.

An opportunity to do better

Sometimes it is easy to get frustrated with someone who is not following your instructions. Trust me, your kids will NOT always follow the recipe when cooking with you. I remember one time when Taco Seasoning was used instead of the Seasoned Salt. It was an easy mistake, as the bottle was the same size and color. But I lost my temper. I said some words in anger that did NOT bless my child, but, rather, rained down condemnation of his listening skills and made him feel stupid. How do you recover from that? Well, you do not simply say, 'Oh well, I guess we aren't cooking together again.' I humbled myself and apologized for getting angry over something that is going to turn to poop in just a few hours, anyway, and we ate taco flavored eggs. The eating of the mistake had more of an impact than even the apology. The fact that I would eat the horrible thing that my kid made (and he knew it was bad because he was eating it, too) meant more to him than any lecture about failure to follow instructions.

Make a plan

NOW THAT WE have discussed the various ways of playing and their importance, it is time to make a plan on how to implement some of this into your daily life. If you find yourself lacking in your playfulness and you want to increase it, like anything else in life, you will never improve if you never practice. Grab one of the suggestions you just read and try to implement it. Today. Not tomorrow. Today. You do not have to master any of these suggestions before you move on to trying another.

Sometimes the enormity of the task ahead makes us feel like grasshopper in our own sight. Do not allow your fear to keep you from starting. The children of Israel became afraid when they heard reports that there were giants living in the land they were supposed to claim as their own. They refused to go forward into the Promised Land. So often what we think are giants looming before us are only shadows cast by fearsome mice. Sometimes they are actually giants, but even giants will fall if you strike them in the right place. Assess your 'giant.' What is keeping you from moving forward? Your schedule? Your work load?

Your other time commitments outside the home? Fear of becoming like your own Dad? Fear of not living UP to the standard your Dad set? Maybe you have multiple giants living in the land. Pick one and engage.

Your kids will notice that you are trying. And they will appreciate it. Do not let these precious few years slip by without being a Playful Dad.

For more information contact Stephen at theplayfuldad@gmail.com.

Dear Reader

Dear reader,

We hope you enjoyed reading Playful Dad. Please take a moment to leave a review, even if it's a short one. Your opinion is important to us.

Discover more books by Stephen Floyd at https://www.nextchapter.pub/authors/stephen-floyd

Want to know when one of our books is free or discounted? Join the newsletter at http://eepurl.com/bqqB3H

Best regards,

Stephen Floyd and the Next Chapter Team

About the Author

Stephen Floyd is a polyglot who grew up in Arizona, learning Spanish and French concurrently. After getting a Bachelor of Arts in Interdisciplinary Humanities, he enlisted in the U.S. Army and became an interrogator, learning Russian at the Defense Language Institute. When it became clear that peacekeepers would be needed to enforce the Dayton Accords in Bosnia, he was ordered to learn Serbo-Croatian and went to Bosnia for an entire year.

Upon returning from that crucial experience he and his wife Erin decided that he should get out of the Army and stay in Alaska, where they have now lived since arriving in 1994, raising their seven children to love God and each other.

Having worked as a Youth Pastor, a school bus driver and as a local radio announcer for 17 years, he got to know Fairbanks in a variety of ways, from the streets to the people to the nightlife and business environment.

Stephen currently works in a guest services position for Northern Alaska Tour Company where he actually gets to use his French, Spanish, Russian, Serbian, and fledgling Chinese. He also has a full studio in his basement, where he records audiobooks.

Lightning Source UK Ltd.
Milton Keynes UK
UKHW020831151220
375245UK00004B/821

9 781715 999483